Blaze™

Dear Reader,

I've been anxiously waiting to tell Charles Roussel and Nanette Vicknair's story, and from the e-mails and letters I've received, I know you've been waiting to read it! Well, here it is, and I must say that I was thrilled to finally let all of you know the truth behind the tension that has existed between these two characters for twelve years.

THE SEXTH SENSE miniseries is near and dear to my heart. So naturally, the eldest Vicknair (not to mention the most complex of them all) has warranted a spot as one of my all-time favorite characters. Nanette was a high-spirited teen when she met sexy, dashing Charles Roussel. And like any teenager, she let her heart and her hormones lead her into a relationship that, in her mind, was "till death do us part." Unfortunately, it almost never turns out that way, and Nanette's relationship was no different. Her heart was broken.

But now, twelve years later, the guy she never got over is back. And he's making it a point to torment her—body and soul—on a regular basis.

I hope you enjoy *Live and Yearn*—Nanette and Charles's story—as well as all the other tales in THE SEXTH SENSE miniseries.

Please visit my Web site, www.kelleystjohn.com, to win a fabulous New Orleans vacation giveaway, learn the latest news about my recent and upcoming releases, and drop me a line. I love hearing from readers!

Happy reading!

Kelley St. John

LIVE AND YEARN
Kelley St. John

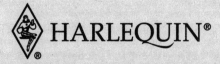

HARLEQUIN®

TORONTO • NEW YORK • LONDON
AMSTERDAM • PARIS • SYDNEY • HAMBURG
STOCKHOLM • ATHENS • TOKYO • MILAN • MADRID
PRAGUE • WARSAW • BUDAPEST • AUCKLAND

ISBN-13: 978-0-373-79425-6
ISBN-10:   0-373-79425-8

LIVE AND YEARN

www.eHarlequin.com

Printed in U.S.A.

ABOUT THE AUTHOR

Kelley St. John's previous experience as a senior writer at NASA fueled her interest in writing action-packed suspense, and she also enjoys penning steamy romances and quirky women's fiction. St. John is a two-time National Readers' Choice Award winner and was elected to the board of directors for Romance Writers of America. Visit her Web site at www.kelleystjohn.com.

Books by Kelley St. John
HARLEQUIN BLAZE
325—KISS AND DWELL
337—GHOSTS AND ROSES
349—SHIVER AND SPICE
397—FIRE IN THE BLOOD
409—BED ON ARRIVAL

To the amazing, talented group
at the Writing Playground:
Problem Child (Kimberly Lang), Instigator
(Kira Sinclair), Angel (Danniele Worsham),
Smarty Pants (Alexandra Frost) and the
Playground Monitor (Marilyn Puett).
Check them out at www.writingplayground.com.

(P.S. If you haven't already purchased
Kira Sinclair's debut Harlequin Blaze novel,
Whispers in the Dark, go buy it—now!
And watch for more remarkable debuts
from this group. They're going places!)

Introduction

DEEP IN THE HEART OF THE BAYOU, the Vicknair plantation holds a notable place amid the winding curves of Louisiana's formidable River Road. Though the force of hurricane Katrina left the once mighty plantation in the worst physical state it's seen in its two hundred years, the home still proudly stands, its namesake family keeping vigil over its survival as diligently as a loving spouse residing at a soul mate's sickbed.

Surrounded by cane fields and showcased by a magnolia-lined driveway, the home would seem worthy of salvation based on its heritage alone. But there is another reason to save the noteworthy estate from the demolition currently claiming so many of Louisiana's antebellum homes post-Katrina. The Vicknair plantation doesn't merely provide sanctuary for the living—it offers a much-needed sanctuary…for the dead.

Since they first moved to St. Charles Parish nearly two hundred years ago, each generation of the Vicknair family has aided wayward spirits who have difficulties crossing over, helping them find out what's wrong and make it right, so they can find their way through to the other side.

The newest generation understands their duty to continue the family tradition *and* protect their secret. The youngest Vicknairs, now predominantly in their twenties, help spirits on a regular basis, perfecting their talent with every crossing.

Nanette, Tristan, Gage, Monique, Dax and Jenee, the six cousins currently performing Vicknair medium duty, realize that when a lavender-tinted envelope materializes on the infamous tea service in the plantation's sitting room, it's time to help a spirit. Their grandmother Adeline Vicknair may be long dead, but she still wants her assignments handled in a timely manner.

Thankfully, her grandchildren know to heed her call and to follow the simple rules associated with helping spirits, rules that have been handed down from generation to generation. Most of those rules are easy to follow, some, such as the no-touching rule, even offer a bit of leeway. True, mediums are not supposed to touch spirits; however, as the current Vicknair mediums have learned, the rules say nothing about a spirit touching a medium.

Nanette Vicknair is the most individualistic of all Vicknair cousins currently serving medium duty, which is only to be expected. At thirty, she's the oldest. She's also the only medium without siblings, not that it's been a huge hardship, since she's as close to all of her cousins, and their spouses, as she would be to biological siblings. Nanette is also the only single Vicknair left. Single. As in, not married, engaged or involved. At all. And she has no desire to be, not since Charles Roussel effectively ruined her trust in men twelve years ago. Back then, he took something from her—or rather, she gave it to him—that could never be replaced. Now he's threatening to take away something else she treasures. Her home.

Twelve years ago, Nanette gave Charles her virginity. She'll be damned if she'll give him anything else.

Prologue

NANETTE VICKNAIR LISTENED TO the familiar sound of crunching gravel in the driveway, easy to hear since the front door of the plantation home had been open all day in an attempt to vent the drywall dust produced by her male cousins. She recognized the soft purr of the engine before exiting the kitchen, heading toward the front door and seeing Charles Roussel's black Mercedes. Again.

The parish president had been by their home three times today already, and each time, Nanette had warned him to not return. To her family, she hoped it appeared as though she was perturbed with him for hindering their progress. But Nanette knew the truth. She'd effectively fought off his charming advances, and the pull he had on her libido, for the past three years, ever since she'd learned that her first lover—and the first guy who'd ever broken her heart—was the primary person who'd decide whether their home would remain standing. Charles was also head of the historical society, the group that determined whether those homes damaged by Hurricane Katrina were worth preserving.

Roussel had used that position to continually stop by Nanette's home under the guise of checking their progress, but while Nan's cousins might believe that was the reason for his way-too-often visits, Nanette knew better. He was

trying to break down her resistance. Trying to charm the
pants off of her—literally—and heaven help her, he was
getting closer and closer to his goal. She was naked for him
every night in her dreams—how long could she hold off
finding herself the same way in reality, if he kept coming
around and driving her sexually deprived body into a
lustful fog?

And Nan didn't want to lose control of her senses to
Charles Roussel. Well, okay, maybe her libido did, but her
brain—and her heart—had been there before and didn't
want to travel that road again. It was a damned rocky road,
and one that she hadn't gotten over since she'd first crossed
it twelve years ago. Before that summer, she'd been known
as the "wild child" of the Vicknair clan. "The Adeline
Vicknair of the future," some folks had said, referring to
her grandmother's fiery spirit, a spirit that Nanette had in-
herited and proudly shown off to the world, until that
summer. Ever since then, she'd fought for control of that
impulsive spirit and she'd succeeded.

Then Charles had returned to Louisiana and, like before,
brought out her "wild child." Only this time, all it wanted
to do was throttle him.

Today, Nanette's emotions were already running rampant
due to the impending deadline for finishing the repairs on the
house. She didn't have the strength or the wherewithal to fight
her natural attraction for Charles. And damn it, he'd noticed.
He'd never been to her home so many times in one day, and
the black Mercedes in her driveway said he wasn't done yet.
Obviously, he could tell she was caving, that each and every
time he got near, she wanted to throw her memories of the
past away and climb on top of him. Right here. Right now.

One look at that gorgeous face, at the wicked twinkle in his eye, and Nanette knew that he saw straight through her. She wanted him, and he knew it.

But she wasn't going to admit it. She *was* going to make certain he left for good this time. She had to. Or she'd find herself naked with the enemy before the day ended.

She took a deep breath and exited the house while Chantelle, Celeste and Jenee watched her from their position on the foyer's stairs. They'd been replacing and refinishing steps all day and were taking a well-deserved breather to enjoy glasses of sweet tea. Their timely break allowed them a front-row seat for the confrontation Nanette was planning with the parish president. But Nanette didn't care. Maybe that'd give her the backbone she needed to tell Charles what to do with his helpful visits. Instead of telling him that what she really wanted him to do was her.

"I thought I told you not to come back," she said, snarling for good measure as she neared the gorgeous Cajun. He'd already gotten out of the car and was leaning against the door, and she could tell by the smirk on his face that he knew he looked good. Then again, he probably knew he looked good doing just about anything. Walking, standing, talking, breathing….

"And I believe I told you that I wanted to take you out to dinner, to discuss your family's options with the house," he said smoothly. Confidently. Cockily.

Nanette gathered her composure, and put clothes back on the image of him that she kept all too handy in her mind. She continued her stride toward him as though she didn't feel her pulse growing more erratic merely because she was getting closer to him. And she couldn't forget that her cousins were probably watching. Although they'd asked her repeatedly whether she and Charles had a history, she'd denied it. No way did she want them to know that the parish president had been her first, or that she'd never gotten over him, even after all these years. She simply wasn't the type of person to share; that quality belonged to Jenee, Monique, Celeste or Chantelle, but never Nanette. She wasn't the rose-colored glasses or the kiss-and-tell type, and she hadn't been in quite a while. Twelve years, to be exact. And the change had been due to this man, smiling at her as though in his mind, she was naked, too.

Nanette wished he'd never seen her that way. Touched her that way. Kissed her all over…that way.

But he had. And he'd done it all very well.

"You must be three crawfish short of a pound to think I'd go out to dinner with you, Roussel, for any reason," she said, loud enough for the eavesdroppers on the steps to hear.

He grinned, and that sinful devil's dimple in his left cheek winked at her. As always, that dimple made her remember how it felt to slip her tongue in that tiny indentation…and run her tongue across lots of other parts of Charles Roussel.

"Nanette, I know how much you enjoy fighting, and hell, I like it, too, seeing you get all hot and worked up and excited," he said, his voice lower now, as though he knew her family might be, and probably were, listening. "But I don't want to fight anymore. Let me have dinner with you, *chère.* I really do want to discuss your family's options, and then, if you're willing, I'd like to talk about *it.*"

She swallowed, glanced toward the house and saw that the three women sitting on the stairs were busy sipping their tea and chatting. Not listening to this exchange, thank goodness. "About *it?*" she questioned.

"About the past, and our future. It's still here, that connection between us, and there's a lot more to what went on back then than you realize, *chère.* I know I pissed you off, but if you'd give me a chance to talk to you about it, instead of sending me away at every opportunity, I think you'd see that things aren't always what they seem. And that I still want you. That I always have." He stepped closer to her with each sentence, and before Nanette had a chance to process his motive for approaching, and her own natural response to it—backing away—he had her pinned against his car.

He placed his hands against hers and clasped them. Nanette was too shocked to stop him, or she didn't want to. At the moment, she wasn't sure which. But in any case, she now found herself against the car, her hands beside her shoulders as Charles Roussel held them in place, and as he held her body in place…with his.

It'd been a long time, way too long, since she'd felt the power of a man, the heat of a man, melting her resistance away. Charles's smoky eyes were focused on hers, and his mouth was so close, so right, that she simply couldn't do anything but…let him do whatever he wanted.

His mouth found hers, and Nanette lost her last ounce of willpower, opening her lips in voracious invitation, burning to feel his tongue slip inside, to feel some part of Charles Roussel joining with her, the way they'd joined so long ago. He was hot, fiery, igniting everything within her that screamed for more. Every emotion she'd kept locked up for so long.

Trapped. Trapped inside *because* of this man.

"No way!" Chantelle's exclamation, echoing from her position on the stairs, slammed Nanette with a hard dose of reality. Yes, she physically wanted Roussel. But emotionally, there was no way in hell she could handle him again. And she had to stop this. Now.

Determined, Nanette wriggled from his embrace, took an off-balanced step away, then reared back and put everything she had into slapping him.

"I was right," he said smugly, rubbing his cheek where she'd hit him.

She needed to get inside the house. She needed to get away. She needed…to know what he was referring to. Flustered, she panted, "Right?"

"You still want me, Nanette Vicknair, even though you don't *want* to want me—and you know I still want you, even more than back then."

Her mouth opened, but no words came out.

"Say yes, Nan. Go to dinner with me tonight. Let's talk about what went wrong back then. I have something I need to tell you, and I'm tired of playing this cat-and-mouse game. Listen, sometimes I let personal situations interfere with political decisions. Hell, all politicians do—it's the nature of the beast. But I shouldn't have done it this time, not when your house is at stake. And I don't think you could even understand why I did it, unless I have a chance to explain. Let me do that, Nan, tonight. I messed up, and I want to get it right." His smile crooked up, and that devil's dimple dipped in. Nanette's panties were instantly drenched with desire. Not good. "I know you want to," he added.

Nanette took a deep breath, struggled to finally gain her

composure, then said softly, "Obviously you don't know me as well as you think, Charles. Because if you did, you'd know that I never make the same mistake twice."

1

NANETTE VICKNAIR EYED HER BED with equal parts anxious trepidation and heightened exhilaration. Trepidation, because ever since that impromptu kiss from Charles Roussel two weeks ago, she hadn't been able to sleep without repeating the experience in her dreams.

And exhilaration for the same reason.

She *needed* a restful night of sleep, and she hadn't had one since Roussel had pressed her against his car and made her momentarily forget who she was, where she was, or what *he* was—a first-class jerk. Tomorrow was the first day of school at Gramercy High, and an exhausted English teacher would be easy prey for a fresh group of ninth graders, many of whom would test her limits from the get-go. She loved her job, loved the teens she taught, but the first day of high school—and particularly, their first day in her class—was one that established the groundwork for all the days that followed. Having a fitful night of sleep due to dreaming about marathon sex sessions with a man she despised wouldn't keep her on top of her game.

Yet, climbing under the covers, Nanette knew there was nothing in the world she could do to stop it. She stretched and yawned, tried to keep her eyes open a little longer and make sure she was as tired as she could be. She'd worked on the house all day; presumably she should drop off to a dead sleep and not remember a thing until morning.

Like that would happen.

Her vision blurred; she couldn't fight the inevitable any longer. Unfortunately, before her eyes slid shut, they focused on the only item that adorned her wall, a framed poster that she should have thrown away years ago. Twelve years ago. The festival portrayed on that poster came to life in her mind. The Ferris wheel, the carousel and off to the side, barely noticeable to most people but dominating the scene to Nan—the house of mirrors. She yawned again, knowing that her thoughts of that poster, and of everything it symbolized, would now control her night.

So much for a restful sleep.

Sighing deeply, she nestled her head into the pillow and didn't fight the pull any longer. It'd happen tonight, like it always did. Whether in a fantasy, or a memory, Charles Roussel would gain control like he always did....

She'd been eighteen; he'd been twenty-two. Nanette had worn a red dress, customary attire for Red-Hot Night at the Old Louisiana Fair grounds. But she hadn't worn the dress for the fair; she'd worn it for Charles Roussel. Charles's grandparents had owned the plantation next to the Vicknair plantation and many of Nanette's teen fantasies had been inspired by their oldest grandson, who'd spent a good deal of time working in their cane fields. Nanette's third-floor bedroom had offered a perfect vantage for watching him labor, shirtless and beautiful, on those hot Louisiana summers.

Eventually, she'd worked up the nerve to venture over to the Roussel property and speak to the object of her affection. Then she'd learned that he wasn't only gorgeous, he was also incredibly charming, particularly when he smiled and that cute dimple dipped in his left cheek.

Nanette's fantasies had quickly turned from dreams of first kisses to much more. And after he'd left for Mississippi State and she'd only seen him in the summers, her desire for the boy—man—next door had only increased. She'd wanted to win his heart and become Mrs. Charles Roussel. They'd have three kids, two boys and a girl, and live in the Vicknair plantation or the Roussel plantation, if he'd rather.

By eighteen, she'd decided it was time to make something happen. Charles was taking a summer break between obtaining his bachelor's degree and starting the master's program at Mississippi State, and after five years of loving him from a distance, Nanette had finally captured his attention as more than a kid. The way he'd looked at her that summer told her he finally saw her the way she wanted, as a woman. And if everything went the way she planned, Charles Roussel would be her first lover.

She was more than ready.

"I've always liked the carousel, but never as much as right now." His voice was deep, much deeper than it'd been earlier tonight, and the warmth of his breath tickled her ear as he nudged her hair out of the way.

Scents of the fairgrounds, sweet cotton candy and heavily buttered popcorn, joined Charles's tantalizing musk scent and made Nanette light-headed, euphoric.

The carousel continued to circle, blending their surroundings into a colorful blur, so she found it even easier to focus on one thing, the man sitting behind her and softly kissing her neck. "I'm glad you're here with me, Nanette."

They'd been together every night since she'd first seen him at the Fourth of July fireworks on the levee, and it was nearly mid-August, not long before he'd leave again for Mississippi State. Nanette pushed that thought away. She didn't want anything negative getting in the way tonight, not when she'd made up her mind.

After a generous amount of time had passed, the music softened to a lull, and the carousel stopped. She sat in front of Charles on the black stallion and felt a distinctive hardness against her behind. Charles wouldn't climb off this horse with ease. She twisted in the seat and smiled. Charles didn't say a word, but his face told her that he knew she'd felt the hard length between his thighs.

"Are you scared, Nanette?"

She wasn't going to pretend that he was talking about the merry-go-round. And she wasn't going to lie, either. "No, I'm—" She tried to find the right word. Excited? Eager? Nervous? "I'm ready."

Charles's gray eyes had deepened to a smoldering storm, and Nanette gasped when he nudged his hips forward, deliberately pressing that impressive bulge against her. "Let's ride again." The warm words teased her ear and sent a shiver down her arms. He must have noticed. He brought his hands to her shoulders, then rubbed them down to her wrists, and back up again.

Nanette's shivering only intensified. She'd never felt desire quite like this, and she didn't know how to go about telling him what she wanted, what she needed.

She vaguely noticed that the fair was closing; one by one, the lights at each of the booths dimmed, while the carousel continued to circle. Nanette leaned back against Charles, listened to his laughter as the breeze blew her hair into his face, then felt his hand gently move the strands to one side so he could nuzzle her neck. The warm air was perfect, the starlit sky was perfect, the man with her was…perfect. This was her dream. It was happening now, and she wanted to enjoy every second as much as possible. Which meant she shouldn't ask any questions about the future. She shouldn't risk ruining what was about to happen.

But Nanette, being Nanette, couldn't resist.

"Charles?"

"Mmm?" He nipped her earlobe, and his hands slowly eased from her arms to the tops of her legs.

She was suddenly very aware of the breeze, lifting the hem of her dress above her knees as the carousel turned. It was warm and intensely erotic, as were his hands, gliding down her thighs and causing the whisper-soft fabric of her dress to rub against her legs in a very interesting way. She heard a soft sound, and realized it'd come from her throat. She swallowed, then tried again. "Charles?"

His hands paused in their progress. "It's okay, *chère.* I've just wanted you, wanted to touch you, for so damn long. For years, if I'm going to be honest."

"Years?"

He exhaled thickly. "Oh, *chère,* you were so tempting, but so young. And now—"

"Now I'm not too young," she whispered.

"No, and I've fought how much I want you, Nanette Vicknair, for a very long time. I'm afraid it's hard for me to hold back. But I won't rush you."

No. He'd misunderstood, and Nanette wasn't advanced enough in all of this to know how to straighten things out.

But she did have something to ask him, something that would help her decide, help her know, how far this should go.

"Will you come back?"

When he didn't readily respond, she added nervously, "I mean, are you going to stay away again while you're at school, or do you think—is there any reason that might find you coming back more often?"

She felt his smile against her neck. "Nanette, I'll admit I didn't plan to come back until Christmas, and then again at the end of the year, like I've been doing."

"But?" she asked, hoped.

"But after spending so much time with you, *chère,* getting to know you even more—" he paused "—wanting you even more... I won't stay away. I can't. I don't know if I'll make it back every weekend, but I'll come as often as I can. If that's what you want. Whatever you want, tell me. I just want to be with you, *chère.*"

"I want to be with you here."

"At the fair?" he asked, his surprise evident. But Nanette heard something else in his tone, too—excitement. Excitement for her.

"Yes," she said, tingling all over from the rush of doing something so unexpected, so wild. She didn't want to wait, didn't want to drive to the levee or even the cane fields nearby. And she didn't want her first time to be in a car. She wanted it to be unique, something they would always remember. She scanned the fairgrounds and saw the perfect place. "In there." She pointed, and he looked toward the place she'd indicated. "What do you think?"

He whistled. "Hell."

"Too risky?" she asked, disappointed.

"No, *chère*. Perfect."

They waited for the fairgrounds to clear, everyone moving to the fields nearby to watch the fireworks customary on the last night of the fair. Then they snuck back into the darkened grounds and headed to the mirrored house.

"Hey, what do you two think you're doing? The fair is closed."

Nanette turned toward the older man. She didn't want anything to ruin this moment, this night. She *wouldn't* let anything ruin it. "I think I left my keys in there," she lied. "Can we go look?"

The man tilted his head skeptically. "That so?" He looked at Charles.

Charles withdrew his wallet, fished out several bills. "Tell you what. I know people have to pay to go in, so let me pay for us to go search for her keys. How much time will this get us?"

The guy fingered through the bills. "Hell, this is more than I made all night."

"So how much time?" Charles asked.

"Stay as long as you need," he said, his gray brows high. Then he paused. "Another fifty and I won't come back until after the fireworks."

Charles handed him the cash. "Thanks."

Laughing, Nan and Charles dashed into the mirrored house.

"You were pretty quick with the lost keys thing," he said.

She giggled, holding his hand as they moved deeper into the maze of mirrors. "You were pretty quick to literally buy more time."

He grinned. "Just polishing up on my future attorney skills."

"Planning to pay off judges?"

"Planning to ask for more time when I need it," he answered. "And we'll need plenty of time, *chère*."

They finally stopped, far enough inside that they weren't easily visible from the outer walls. Without the bright lights of the fair, the glass ceiling was even more magical, spilling moonlight in that reflected their images on the surrounding walls.

Charles turned her so her back was against his front, and she felt that hard presence against her bottom. "Look at us, Nanette."

Their reflection was mirrored from all directions, and she gasped at the thrill of what they were about to do. With all of the mirrors, there was no way she wouldn't see *everything*. No way she wouldn't remember everything.

Charles's hands gently eased her thighs apart, then slid the fabric of her skirt up to her waist. His mouth nipped along her jaw, and Nanette tilted her face, bringing her mouth to meet his, then she hummed her contentment when his tongue parted her lips while his fingers slipped inside her panties.

She was wet, very wet, and he obviously noticed, because he also hummed his satisfaction when he touched her there.

"Nanette," he said, easing one finger inside her opening while she closed her eyes and tried to tattoo everything her body was feeling on her mind, so she could revisit this night, this moment, forever. "Have you ever been with a man, Nanette? Slept with a man?"

She wasn't going to play games now. There was no

reason to hide anything from him. He'd know soon enough, anyway. She shook her head. "No. I was waiting…for you."

If possible, his erection seemed to grow even harder as it pressed against her bottom, and Nanette wanted more than anything to learn what that felt like, to have that part of him within her, deep within her, right where he was touching her now.

His thumb slid up her folds and rubbed that tiny, burning spot, and she gasped against his throat, her body on fire and needing to set that fire free, let it go.

"What about this?" he asked, and she sensed his possessive tone. He'd be her first, her last, her only. This night was the beginning of forever, *their* forever. She was eternally glad that she'd waited. "Has anyone ever done *this* to you before, Nanette? Has anyone ever made you come?"

She didn't know how to answer the question. Her mind was all foggy, in a hot and heated pre-orgasmic existence that could barely put two thoughts together. Should she tell him the truth? Would he think she was strange? Or was it normal? She'd never really asked anyone, and had never thought it'd be a topic of discussion, especially not in the midst of her body losing complete control at the beckoning of Charles's talented fingers. "I—I—" She was so close it hurt. Why couldn't he just keep going, and faster, and let her have that climax that was almost there, and then they'd talk about this later?

"Nanette." His fingers slowed, and she looked at their reflection. Her skirt above her waist. His hand inside her panties. She wanted, needed, burned for more, but he was slowing down. She wanted to scream.

"Has anyone ever made you come?" he asked.

It was embarrassing, but it was the truth, and maybe if she told him, he'd keep going. "Only me. I've done it," she said breathlessly. "A lot. At night. And every time...*every* time...I think of you."

His mouth captured hers almost brutally, and Nanette welcomed his hungry assault. She'd never told anyone something so intimate, so private, but evidently her uncontrollable desire for him, the fact that she'd already had him, many times, in her mind, made him even more eager to give her the real thing. He continued kissing her, while his fingers, blessedly, resumed stroking her into oblivion. And when he felt her body tense, and he knew that she was about to let go, he claimed her scream with his kiss, until her body shook with the power of her release.

She turned in his arms, her entire body on fire. He'd given her an orgasm, but she wanted more. And she wasn't going to stop until she got it. She took her hands to his waist, quickly unbuttoned his pants and slid the zipper down. Then her hands slipped inside and found that hot, thick heat that'd been teasing her senses all night. She stroked his length, marveled at the size and wondered how all of that could fit inside of her.

But she didn't want to merely wonder. She wanted to know. "Now, Charles," she said, panting from her need. "I want you now. Don't you dare say no."

"Trust me, *chère*. With you *no* never enters my mind."

They undressed frantically, hungrily, eager to have what they both craved. Nanette barely registered him rolling a condom down his length before he lifted her, placed her back against one of the mirrored walls and finally slid inside.

She sucked in her breath as her body struggled to take him all in and a sharp pain pierced her.

He stopped, held still, and she looked at their reflection and saw…he was only halfway in.

"*Chère,* we can stop. I don't ever want to hurt you."

"No, please don't stop, Charles. I just want to—watch."

He followed her gaze to the walls, saw the erotic image they created reflected all around them, and pushed all the way in.

Nanette watched, spellbound, as he guided her up, then slid her back down, slowly up and down, while her body adjusted to the tender invasion and his penis became more slick, more wet. She saw the evidence of her lost virginity on his length, and she suddenly felt terribly inexperienced.

"Charles, is this—" She swallowed. "Do I feel good for you?" Her attention was on the same thing as his, the images of their naked bodies surrounding them.

"*Chère,* you feel *perfect* for me," he said hoarsely, and she noticed beads of sweat on his brow and a definite strain for control on his face.

Nanette knew he was trying not to hurt her, trying to keep things slow for her, but that wasn't what she wanted. She wanted to see him lose control. "Charles, I need, I want—" A loud boom signaled the fireworks had started.

"What do you want, *chère?*"

She moved her hips to slide up his length, then back down. The pain was gone now, and the pleasure was returning with fervor. "I want harder. Faster. I want to come again. Make me come, Charles."

"Oh, *chère,*" he said, his voice a growl as he gripped

her hips and matched her building rhythm, thrusting deep, deep inside. The tension spiraled, burning wildly through her.

Nanette focused on the images around them, Charles pushing into her, their naked bodies in the throes of passion. The pressure built and built, until Charles's entire body tensed and he pushed even deeper, and the fireworks exploded, not only above them, but within them, searing this perfect moment in her mind forever.

Nanette woke with her head thrashing on the pillow, her heart pounding frantically in her chest, the same way it had that night so long ago. "Charles, please." She knew he wasn't here, knew it was merely a dream that had gotten her to this state again, but she also knew that the only way to get where she wanted to go…was to think of him. And so, she pictured him, his dark hair in waves over his forehead, that devil's dimple winking at her with his sexy smile. Gray eyes turning the color of storm clouds as he grew more and more aroused, his prominent, bold erection probing against her intimate center the same way it had back then, the night when she'd given him everything.

"I just want to be with you… I don't ever want to hurt you."

She'd believed those words, believed him. And even though he'd never come back for her and even though he'd hurt her more than anyone else, she still couldn't get him out of her mind, out of her heart, out of her bed.

She wanted him now as much as she wanted him then. More. She was so close. Opening her eyes, she kicked the sheets off the bed and spread her thighs farther, moved her fingers over her clitoris until she felt a damp trickle against her thighs. Why couldn't she get there without him? Why did it have to be Charles Roussel in order for her to come?

She didn't know, and at the moment, she didn't care. She needed…release. And damn it, she needed him. Her chest heaved with erratic breaths as she let her eyes slide closed and imagined him entering her, joining her, thrusting into her with every bit of power he possessed. Nanette accepted every thrust, her hips pumping upward from the bed, her fingers moving wildly to take her where she so desperately wanted to go.

And finally—finally—she soared over the edge… with him.

When her pulse stilled and her breathing had steadied, she slowly opened her eyes, then rolled over and rubbed her cheeks against the pillow to dry her tears. Then she glanced again at the sole painting centered on her wall, at the tiny building that was the house of mirrors. "Damn you, Charles Roussel. Damn you straight to hell."

2

NANETTE TOSSED HER LOADED TOTE on the kitchen table, fell into a chair and dropped her head into her hands. She felt…defeated. The first day of school was over, and the kids had been as sharp as ever. Sharper. There was no fooling fourteen- and fifteen-year-olds into thinking that she ran the show when she hadn't slept soundly for more than a couple of hours, and only after she'd mentally *had* Charles Roussel no fewer than three times.

No matter how often she'd warned her students to keep their talking to a minimum during their assignment, the low mumbles had grown louder and louder, and with her lack of sleep, Nanette had heard it in the same manner as fingernails on a chalkboard.

They were supposed to write a short essay about what they'd done over the summer. The assignment was meant to be an icebreaker—a way to get them back into the habit of writing again. If she could've maintained order, they wouldn't have continually chatted throughout the writing process, and Nanette wouldn't have eventually blown her top and issued them a ridiculously large amount of homework on their very first day of school. She could only imagine the comments from the parents at the next PTA meeting.

But what was done was done, and she'd regroup tomorrow and repair the damage. Tonight, one way or another, she had to get some rest. Maybe a trip to the store for some sleeping pills would keep Charles Roussel out of her mind—and out of her bed.

Yeah, right.

The hinges on the swinging door to the hall creaked as someone entered the kitchen. Nanette didn't bother looking up to see who it was.

"Rough first day, huh?" Jenee asked.

Nanette pushed an abundance of black hair out of her face and squinted one eye open to view her youngest cousin and her fiancé, Nick Madere, entering the kitchen.

"You have no idea. The kids were tough, but I was tougher. And right now, I'm thinking that might not have been such a great thing." She yawned so broadly her jaw popped. "What're you guys doing here?" Nanette could tell from their clothing, covered in drywall dust, that they'd been working on the house, but she hadn't realized they'd planned to spend Monday at the plantation. The family always worked together on the weekends, but weekdays were typically for, well, work.

Nick wrapped an arm around Jenee and grinned. "I've got to head back to Virginia tomorrow to train the new guy, the last order of business before I leave my job there and start full-time in New Orleans. We'll work a case together so he can get the full picture of his duties, and that could take a while, at least a couple of weeks. So I asked Jenee if she wanted to take a day off from the shelter and the two of us come out here and help with the house while I'm still in town. You've got so much to do before your inspection, and I feel bad about being gone during your last few weeks."

Nick had previously worked at the National Center for Missing and Exploited Children, but was taking a job with the New Orleans Police Department helping locate missing children locally and to be near Jenee.

Jenee kissed his cheek with no mind that it was covered in white dust. Nick laughed at her white-tinted lips and brushed them clean with his thumb. They were so in love that it…hurt. Nanette wanted a love like that. Actually, she just wanted to be *able* to love again, in spite of the way Charles Roussel had bruised her heart so many years ago.

"We finished the drywall in the dining room," Jenee announced.

"And thanks to Ryan and his ghost, we also got started on the crown molding," Nick added.

Nanette's eyes widened at that, suddenly a little more awake. Ryan Chappelle had been a ghost himself not that long ago, until he'd married Nan's cousin Monique and consequently got another chance at life on this side. Now, like every other Vicknair spouse, he also helped lost spirits find their way. So the fact that he had a ghost with him wasn't surprising; the fact that his ghost was putting up crown molding at the plantation, however, was. "Ryan and his ghost?"

"I know. It seemed strange to me, too," Jenee admitted, still squeezing an arm around Nick while she spoke as though she couldn't get close enough to him. "Apparently, Ryan's latest assignment wanted to 'leave something for the world to remember him by' before he crossed over to the light. And evidently, he was some kind of carpenter. So, before he crosses, he wants to design the molding in a home that will be around a while." Jenee grinned. "Ours."

"What's he going to do if Charles Roussel gets his way, and this place gets put on that demolition list in six weeks?" Nanette asked, hating that, once again, Charles was dominating her thoughts. Three years ago, when she'd first learned that the newly elected parish president would be steering the historical society—and determining which houses stood post-Katrina—Nanette had felt like she'd been given an emotional death sentence. Charles had only been back in Louisiana for a year at that time, and she'd successfully avoided him throughout each day of those first twelve months. But after Katrina, she'd had no way of avoiding him if she wanted to save the family home. No way at all.

Jenee frowned. "Nan, you must be tired. That's the first time I've ever heard you sound as though you don't think the historical society will give us the funding we need to keep the house standing. We've made a huge dent in the repairs, and the society said that they take that into consideration when deciding which houses should receive funding."

"I'm sorry." Nanette instantly recalled the day the society had shown up at her door after Katrina, and the moment she'd seen Charles again, for the first time after all these years.

"You need to sleep," Jenee continued.

"Yeah, I do." Nan didn't want to be a downer for the rest of the family now. Jenee was right; she was tired. Very tired. And cranky. And in need of sex, *real* sex. The kind she hadn't had in longer than she cared to admit. "You're right. We're going to get everything done in time. And hopefully, by the time they come, only the biggest obstacles will need repairing, the right side of the house and the columns, right?"

"Right," Jenee said, grinning again, and obviously forgiving Nanette for her sudden negativity.

"Well, since I am heading out tomorrow, I think we're going to call it a day and go back to my place," Nick said, then he smiled at Jenee, and she practically melted. No doubt that they wanted to have some alone time before his departure. Nick had wasted no time purchasing a house near the battered women's shelter where Jenee worked. The place wasn't overly large, but it was beautiful and suited them.

Again, a tinge of something that bordered scarily toward jealousy inched through Nanette, and she swallowed past it. This was her cousin, and she would not begrudge Jenee for having the type of relationship every woman deserved.

The type Nanette also deserved, if she could ever get over Roussel and the effect he had on her. She closed her eyes and saw him standing on her front porch when the committee members had first evaluated her home after the hurricane. "You need me, *chère*," he'd said. "Let me help you." Her response had been something to the effect of when hell froze over—and the battle had begun.

"Nan, okay if we leave?" Jenee asked, and Nan's eyes flew open.

She nodded. "Yeah, you two head on home. We'll miss you on the weekends before the final inspection, Nick, but I do appreciate both of you spending the day here." Good. She sounded normal, composed.

Jenee stepped away from Nick to hug Nan, and Nanette coughed when the action sent a puff of drywall dust straight up her nose. Jenee giggled. "Sorry, Nan."

"No problem." Nanette brushed the white dust from her black shirt and smiled at the two of them.

They started toward the back door, then Jenee stopped and motioned to a stack of envelopes on the counter. "I brought the mail in when we got here, but I never got around to opening it."

"I'll go through it." The majority of the stack would be bills, which the family would divvy up this weekend when they arrived for the regular workday. Although Nanette was the only Vicknair currently residing in the home, they all chipped in to keep things running and to pay for what repairs they could. Regardless of who actually lived in the home, the ghosts visited *all* of the Vicknair mediums here, via Grandma Adeline's sitting room; therefore, they all felt some sense of ownership of the place. Besides, there was no way she could afford this huge house on her tiny teacher's salary.

She waited for Jenee and Nick to leave, then she decided to wade through the mail, separate the bills from the trash and maybe find a magazine that would help her unwind after her frustrating day.

It didn't take but a quick scan to see there wasn't a magazine in the bunch. A couple of mail-order catalogs, but nothing she was interested in, and she tossed those in the trash. Then came the bills. Water bill, gas bill, electric bill…

Her breath caught at the return address on the next envelope.

Charles Roussel, Chairman
River Road Historical Society

"What have you done now, Roussel?" She ran her finger along the edge of the envelope. In her haste, she sliced her skin, and the paper cut left a thin smear of blood in its wake.

Being a Vicknair, Nanette was a big believer in signs.

That stark red streak across the white envelope told her that there was nothing inside this envelope that was going to be good. And if that wasn't enough foreshadowing, *his* name on the outside of the envelope confirmed it.

She withdrew the single sheet of paper with even more apprehension than she withdrew her ghostly assignments from her grandmother's lavender envelopes. Those letters only came from the middle realm, from the other side. This one came straight from hell.

> We regret to inform you that the historical society has identified a need to confirm all decisions for restoration by the first of September. We realize that your initial date for final inspection was the first of October; however, after much discussion and analysis of the plantations still under consideration for historical society funding, we realize that our current sources will only provide funding for half of the homes that have applied for assistance. In order to repair those homes in a timely manner, prior to the upcoming hurricane season, we will make our decisions on the homes to be preserved one month earlier than originally anticipated. Therefore, please be prepared for your final inspection on or before the first of September. If you have any questions regarding this notice, please contact Charles Roussel, Parish President and Historical Society Chairman.

Nanette's exhaustion was forgotten, immediately replaced with white-hot rage. She had no doubt who was behind the rescheduling of final inspections. Roussel knew that if they had to show the home in two weeks, the Vicknair plantation wouldn't be in the top half of homes that received funding. It was still too far off the mark, way too far, compared to some of the other plantations along the levee's edge. They'd taken a bigger hit than most, or perhaps the house simply hadn't withstood the Category 3 winds as well as the others, but in any case, there was no doubt that they weren't ready for that inspection——and that they wouldn't be ready in a measly two weeks. Particularly with all of the Vicknair family working regular jobs, as well. Somehow, they'd have to find time to work on the plantation during the week, which meant taking time off of their jobs.

She couldn't do that. She simply couldn't leave her class to substitute teachers now, not the first two weeks of the school year. There was no way. And Chantelle, Kayla and Jenee were working long hours at the shelter, Celeste was teaching kindergarten, Dax had his pharmaceuticals route, Monique was running her salon, and Ryan's roofing company was as busy as ever. She blinked. Tristan and Gage. They could work more than the rest. Tristan's days at the firehouse varied, and maybe he could get his firemen back here to help out before the inspection. And Gage would work whenever he wasn't on duty at the hospital.

Nanette glared at the letter, wadded it and tossed it toward the trash. It hit the side and bounced off, yet another sign. She shouldn't be worrying about who could work when. They *should* have another six weeks to get every-thing done, the way they'd planned. But, no, Charles Roussel had intervened once again and attempted to make her life a living hell.

He'd been stopping by continually and criticizing their progress, telling them how they'd never get the place finished in time. Now he'd gone one step further, actually eliminating the entire last month of their schedule.

The last time she'd seen the man, he'd shocked her with that kiss. Taking what he didn't have a right to take. Doing what she didn't want him to do.

A tiny whisper at the back of her mind said that wasn't true; she had wanted him to do it, and more.

That intensified her anger.

She stormed across the kitchen, grabbed the cordless phone, then snatched up the wadded paper and unfolded it. Scanning the header, she punched in the number stamped across the top before she had a chance to change her mind.

Turning toward the window, she noticed that in the short time since Nick and Jenee had left, the sky had darkened exponentially, and it'd started to rain. Not a typical rain, but the steady sheets of water that often followed the course of the Mississippi dousing everything in sight. Another accurate depiction of this horrendous day. And she was about to add the icing to the bitter cake by talking to Roussel.

Don't let him rattle you, she silently commanded herself. He knew how to get under her skin, and he apparently enjoyed doing it. But today, Nanette vowed, she wasn't giving him the satisfaction.

She'd had plenty of confrontations with the man, but they'd always occurred with him as the aggressor, showing up at her house and throwing her world off-kilter with his smug, sexy smile, bewitching gray eyes and—*mon Dieu*—that deadly dimple.

Not this time. She wasn't waiting for his appearance before giving him a piece of her mind.

"Charles Roussel's office," the soft voice breathed from the other end of the line. Nanette pictured a blue-eyed blonde, early twenties, big perky boobs, skintight dress. A trophy secretary. One who was probably more than willing to do whatever her gorgeous boss wanted. She suddenly recalled Holly Hunter playing that secretary in *The Firm,* the one who was under the desk and "servicing" her boss. Maybe someone should tell the parish president—that guy got shot.

Nan's blood boiled. "Let me speak to Roussel." She wasn't acknowledging that he even had a first name.

The woman on the line cleared her throat. "I'm afraid President Roussel just left for the day. May I take a message? He'll return your call as soon as he's back tomorrow morning."

"No, I'm not leaving a message. I need to talk to him, and I need to talk to him now." Before her temper had a chance to cool. "He has a cell phone, right?"

Another clearing of the woman's throat, and this time it sounded rather nervous. *Good.* "Yes, ma'am, he does, but I don't typically give that number out. If this is an emergency—"

"It is." Nanette's house was probably being demolished in two weeks because of this bastard so, yes, it was most definitely an emergency. "I need the number now. Either you can give it to me, or I'll get it from his brother, Johnny." Johnny Roussel lived next door to the Vicknair plantation, having moved into the place after his grandparents died. Nanette rarely saw the younger Roussel brother, much less spoke to him, but she assumed throwing out his name wouldn't hurt to get her what she wanted, and she was right.

"Oh, well, no need for that." Trophy secretary was irritated, but Nanette didn't care. "Do you have a pen?"

"I'm ready." Nanette didn't need a pen and paper. She'd be dialing the jerk as soon as she hung up the phone. And immediately after Trophy spouted the number, she disconnected, and did just that.

The phone rang. And rang. And rang. Nanette waited until his voice mail clicked on and that deep, throaty, Cajun, sexy-as-sin voice came on the line. "Charles Roussel. I'm currently unavailable to take your call. Please leave a message."

Nanette fumed. He obviously had caller ID, and he wasn't going to take her call. Or so he thought. She hung up and hit redial.

3

CHARLES ROUSSEL TURNED onto River Road and immediately wished he'd taken Airline Highway. Typical for Louisiana, this storm had come out of nowhere. It hadn't even been sprinkling when he left his office, and now he couldn't see ten feet in front of him as he navigated the road's endless curves. He knew River Road like the back of his hand, but it didn't matter in this downpour, when he couldn't identify one landmark from another, one home from another, and when all the curves seemed to run together and convert the usual picturesque route into a monotonous labyrinth of gray asphalt.

He'd planned to go by his brother's place on the way home and visit with his family while also checking on the progress of the Vicknair plantation. Usually, he could view Nanette Vicknair's place easily from Johnny's side porch, but with this storm, he probably wouldn't even be able to make out their house, much less catch a glimpse of the black-haired beauty that lived there. Which, of course, was his real reason for wanting to visit his brother.

His cell phone rang. Thanking God for the hands-free cradle in his Mercedes, he methodically pressed the button to answer it, careful not to take his eyes off the wet road ahead. "Roussel."

"Paran?"

Charles smiled. Cindy, Johnny's step-daughter, had referred to him by the tender Cajun term for *godfather* ever since she'd become a part of the family. The endearment never failed to touch his heart.

"Hey, Cindy. Everything okay at the office?" When she'd expressed a desire to find an after-school job for some extra cash during her senior year, Charles had wasted no time offering her the receptionist position for the last two hours of every day. The situation had been perfect, since his usual receptionist wanted to spend time with her grandchildren in the afternoons. Cindy loved the job, even if she did get a little nervous at times dealing with members of the parish who were upset over one thing or another. But she was fine-tuning her people skills, and was becoming quite the professional, if he did say so himself.

"Did I hear a beep? Do you have another call?" she asked quickly.

Charles hardly heard the break in the line over the rain beating a wild staccato on his windshield. "Yeah, I think so, but they can leave a message. What did you need?"

"Good, I got to you first," she said, then added, "I'm so glad I've got you on speed dial here, because I gave your number to this woman, and I'm sure that's who's calling you. I know I'm not supposed to give out your cell number, but she said if she didn't get it from me, then she'd get it from Daddy, and I didn't want her calling Daddy, you know, and making him think I wasn't doing my job."

A curve snuck up on him, and Charles gripped the wheel tighter. "It's okay, Cindy. Listen, I don't want you going down River Road to get home. Take Airline as long as you can before cutting over. Or better yet, just hang out at the office until the storm dies down, okay?" The line beeped again. This time he heard it more clearly, but he wasn't getting off the phone until he was certain his godchild wouldn't attempt to drive in this mess.

"Okay. I bet that's her calling again. I hear the beeping. I'm sorry, *Paran*. I shouldn't have given her your number."

"No problem, *petit*. I'll handle the call. You just stay there and stay safe, until the storm passes."

"I love you, *Paran*."

Again, he smiled. "You, too." And the line beeped again. Whoever this woman was, she sure was impatient to talk to him. "Call me when you get home, Cindy."

"I will." She disconnected, and the beeping immediately converted to a shrill ring.

Irritated, Charles answered the phone. "Roussel."

"About time you answered."

Charles felt his blood stir, along with the most dominant part of his anatomy. Have mercy, no other woman affected him like Nanette.

"*Mais*, Ms. Vicknair, to what do I owe the pleasure?" He laid the Cajun on thick. He couldn't help it. Every time he spoke to Nanette, he remembered her gasping so many years ago, telling him that his accent, more than a little thicker than the typical Cajun drawl, made her wet.

Did it still?

"How dare you, Charles!"

Ah, she'd received the letter. He'd rehearsed what he'd say when he saw her, but he hadn't expected her to call. Evidently, the letter had riled her even more than he'd anticipated. "Nanette, the decision to move the deadline up was made by the committee, the entire committee. Contrary to your obvious belief, I'm not the sole person responsible for the decisions they make, and they wanted to begin funding before this year's hurricane season, so we can start working toward saving the homes we can before they are subjected to another storm. By continuing to keep so many homes on the list, we're limiting our chances to restore the ones that are salvageable. The decision had nothing to do with undermining your family's plans."

"It had everything to do with it," she snapped. "No. *You* had everything to do with it. They listen to you, and you know damn well that we need more time in order for this place to be included in the top half of the homes to be restored. That is what this letter states, isn't it? That the historical society will save approximately fifty percent of the plantations that have applied for funds. Right? I'm reading it now, Charles, and it clearly—"

"Nanette," he said, interrupting her current tirade, while also reveling in the fiery spirit that had captivated him so long ago. Fiery spirit, fiery body, fiery woman. If only things had turned out differently way back then, perhaps he could have had the whole package, instead of finding himself only on the receiving end of her fiery venom. *Mon Dieu,* she hated him with a passion. "The society is meeting tomorrow night, and I'm planning to speak to them on your family's behalf."

"You can't expect me to believe that. Not after you've done nothing *but* cause my family trouble ever since you learned your committee had the power to decide whether this place stays or goes."

"You have to believe it. It's the truth." It was. Yes, he'd

enjoyed sparring with her over the past few years. But hell, he hadn't really wanted the place destroyed. He'd merely kept them hanging in the balance to have an excuse to bother the oldest Vicknair. If he couldn't be near her the way he wanted, he'd take what he could get. Besides, fighting with Nanette provided the most exhilarating entertainment he'd had in years. And the last time they'd fought, it had provided more. That kiss. A heated interaction that he couldn't have stopped if he tried. Hell, they'd been building toward it for the entire three years, teetering on the brink of ripping each other to pieces...or ripping off each other's clothing.

If they hadn't been in her driveway, in the light of day, with a good portion of her cousins watching, Roussel suspected some cloth ripping might have occurred two weeks ago. He'd messed up, playing political games to get closer to Nanette, and it had backfired. He was getting closer, but not the way he wanted. And he'd fix that at tomorrow's meeting.

When they'd kissed, he could tell she'd wanted him almost as much as he wanted her. She'd clawed at him and pulled him against her hot, yielding body the same way she had her very first time, when she'd approached sex in the same manner as she approached every other aspect of life—without fear.

But now, he thought he heard a hint of fear in her tone. She seriously thought that he'd take her house away, have it bulldozed to the ground. He shouldn't have let things get this far, to the final inspection. He should have backed the Vicknair plantation personally, instead of personally talking it down, simply because he wanted to tangle with Nanette as long as possible. But he'd straighten everything out at tomorrow's meeting, tell the committee that he'd put the Vicknair plantation at the top of the list of homes that should be salvaged, if for no other reason than the family's longevity in the parish. They'd been here two hundred years, right next to the plantation his family had owned for just as long, where Johnny now lived. Charles frowned. He'd always thought he'd live there, but then his grandparents had passed on when he was still dealing with everything in Mississippi. Johnny had wanted to move his family in and at the time, Charles had no reason to think he'd ever move back home. Or fulfill his dream of living in that house…with Nanette Vicknair by his side.

"Where is the meeting?" Her words were clipped, undeniably driven by anger, and Charles banished thoughts of what might have been.

"It's a private meeting, closed to the public," he said. "And I told you that I would talk to the committee on behalf of—"

"And I'm telling you that I don't believe you. Why would I trust anything you say, Charles? Why?" Her voice cracked on the last word, and he swallowed hard. He'd hurt her, back then and again now. Why *should* she believe him?

"Nanette." Fighting with her was one thing; hurting her was something else entirely. And something that he never intended to do. She'd always seemed so tough, so strong, so thrilled by the battle. He'd never really thought about the fact that he could very well be taking away her will to fight at all. Breaking her spirit. A spirit that had drawn him to her so long ago, and still captured him now. For three long years, he'd tormented her, and why? Because he'd been fighting himself, trying to downplay the truth of his own feelings. After everything that happened in Missis-sippi, he hadn't wanted to desire any woman again, even Nanette. But the truth was…he did. And it was damn time he stopped fighting it.

"When will it be enough?" she asked, and Charles could swear she'd started to cry. "Haven't you hurt my family—haven't you hurt me—enough? And what did I ever do to you but…but…"

Damn. He *had* gone too far this time. "Nanette, I swear, I never meant to—" A small dark shadow caught his atten-tion, something running across the road directly in front of his car. A dog? A *child?* He slammed his foot on the brake, and the car swerved, and a black dog barked loudly as it veered away from the spinning vehicle. Charles turned the wheel into the spin, but the tires went beyond the edge of the pavement, and then everything blurred.

Rain, trees, levee, rain, trees, levee, Nanette yelling something, rain, trees, levee, faster, faster, Nanette yelling his name, rain, trees…nothing.

4

IT WAS AFTER ONE IN THE morning when Gage Vicknair finally emerged through the doors of the Critical Care Unit at Ochsner Hospital to relay Charles Roussel's condition to his family. Nanette's eyes burned, both from lack of sleep and from crying until she simply couldn't cry anymore.

She edged forward in her seat to catch Gage's attention. He'd known she was waiting, had met her briefly when she'd arrived at the hospital, but he couldn't speak to her now. He had to talk to the family first. But he did manage to look her way, and his expression was grim.

Oh, God, Charles was dead. Dead, because of her!

Nanette moved her hand to her mouth, biting down on the side of her fist to keep from wailing aloud. The family didn't need that now. They needed calm, needed peace.

They needed Charles.

What had she done? Why hadn't she considered that he was driving when she'd called him on his cell, and that the majority of his drive home occurred along River Road? Why hadn't she thought about the fact that getting him so worked up with her outburst would take his attention off the treacherous storm, and off that deadly wet road?

She closed her eyes and heard that awful conglomeration of sounds again. Wheels squealing, Charles yelling, the car…crashing.

"Oh, *Paran!*"

The anguished cry forced Nanette's eyes open. After hearing whatever Gage had said, Johnny Roussel's oldest daughter was sagging against her father's side. The pretty girl had said she'd been talking to her uncle right before he crashed, that she'd called him from his office. She'd believed that she'd caused the crash, but the police who'd come from the scene of the accident had assured her that it appeared he'd swerved to keep from hitting something. They assumed an animal of some type had darted in front of Charles's car, and he'd lost control.

Nanette had been sickened to hear that Cindy thought she was responsible because she'd called her uncle while he was driving in the storm. Charles *had* been on the phone with someone at the time of his crash—her. It hadn't been an animal; it had been an irate bitch giving him a hard time while he attempted to navigate River Road in a storm—that had essentially killed him. And Nanette now realized her assumptions about Charles's secretary had been appallingly wrong. She'd been talking to his niece earlier and had jealously treated her as if she was nothing more than a hired tramp. That made Nan feel even guiltier.

Charles's family, consisting of his parents, Johnny and Johnny's wife and kids, hadn't questioned Nanette's unwavering vigil at the hospital. They'd assumed it was because she had been the first person on the scene. Little did they know the reason she'd been the one to find Charles was because *she'd* caused the accident.

As soon as Nan had heard the crash through the line,

she'd grabbed her cell phone and keys and headed into the storm. Charles's secretary—niece—had said he'd gone home for the day, and Nanette had correctly assumed that he'd taken the quickest route, down River Road. She'd found his car less than a mile from her plantation, crumpled in a wet black mass of metal against the levee. Running to the Mercedes, she'd dialed 911 when she'd seen Charles, engulfed by a deployed airbag and covered with blood. It had gushed from a horrid slash that split the lower left side of his face, and it trickled from his mouth and ears. Nan wasn't a doctor, but she knew enough from having Gage as a cousin to know that Charles was in bad shape. Head trauma. Internal injuries. Death? She'd given the 911 operator as much info as she could, then she'd tried to staunch the bleeding until the ambulance came, but it didn't seem to have done any good. He had no color at all upon arrival at the hospital. He'd looked like a man at death's door, and now Nanette feared that he'd passed through that door.

Have mercy, what if she received Charles as a spirit assignment? What if—God forbid—she had to help him cross over, and say goodbye to him for good? For the past twelve years, she'd only conveyed her hatred for him breaking her heart. How hard would it have been to tell him, just once, that she'd longed for him? That she'd never gotten over him? That she wanted him…still?

And now he was gone.

Nanette's gasp ripped from her throat, and Gage turned his attention from the huddled group of crying family members in the hall to her, still sitting in the tiny waiting room where she'd been all night.

He approached her slowly, his face etched in concern

and his usually vivid blue eyes dimmed from the exhaustion that came with a long night of trauma. He wore green scrubs and had a white surgeon's mask bunched at his neck. His surgical cap looked like something that belonged on a beach, a Hawaiian print of blue, orange and yellow tropical flowers. Normally, it'd have made her smile. But not tonight.

"Is he…" She couldn't force the rest of the question through her lips. The word *dead* had never bothered her before. She was a Vicknair, after all, and quite accustomed to dealing with those who'd passed on beyond this realm. More than that, as a Vicknair, she knew that just because a spirit ceased to live on this side, that didn't mean their existence was over. Far from it. But still, the thought of Charles crossing over so young, at merely thirty-four, and before she got to say goodbye, pained her in ways that she couldn't express.

"He's still here," Gage said, reaching for her hand. "But I'll be honest with you, Nan—I don't know for how long." He indicated the Roussel family, huddled in prayer in the hallway. "Come on, let's walk. I'll tell you what I know, and I want you to do the same."

She didn't have to wonder what he meant. Gage knew that she hadn't just happened upon Charles's accident. Gage had seen her, heard her, when she was paranoid that she'd killed him. She'd even told him that it was her fault when she arrived at the hospital. Gage had wasted no time making sure she was out of earshot of nurses, doctors and the police. Then he'd set about calming her down, telling her he would tend to Charles and let her know his condition as soon as possible. Thankfully, Johnny and the rest of Charles's family hadn't yet arrived when Nanette had been going off the deep end. If they'd heard her words to her cousin, they wouldn't have known what to think.

Nan and Gage walked down the hallway. He opened the door to an empty doctor's lounge and pointed toward an enormous coffeemaker. "Two sugars, right?"

She nodded, then sat on the vinyl gold sofa centered on one wall and waited while he filled two foam cups then returned to sit next to her on the couch. She took a sip, and it scalded her tongue. The instant pain reminded her how quickly things could change. Charles had undoubtedly felt pain, too. Nan thought of his beautiful face, sliced open and colorless, and she whimpered into her cup.

"Nan, it doesn't look good. He's on a ventilator now, and his kidneys are barely functioning. Evidently, the steering wheel pressed into his—"

Nanette held up her hand, swallowing past the coffee creeping steadily back up her throat. "No, Gage, please. Don't. I can't listen to the details. Just tell me if he'll make it. No, tell me that he *will* make it, Gage."

One corner of Gage's mouth dipped down, and he shook his head slightly as he spoke. "I can't tell you that, Nan. We've done all we can, but honestly, it doesn't look good."

Her hand trembled, and some of the scalding coffee sloshed over the side and onto her pants. It didn't hurt nearly as bad as her heart.

Gage took her cup and placed it on a table nearby next to his, then leaned forward and took her hands in his. "Nanette, you said you did it. What did you do? You weren't in the car with him, so what makes you think you caused this?"

"I—" She took a deep breath, and gained her courage. "I got a letter from him today, or I mean, from the historical society, saying that they were cutting our time to work on the house by a month. Gage, I was so mad, and I just knew he was behind it. I should have thought about the storm before I called him, but I didn't, and I was so angry. I wouldn't let up. I kept yelling and yelling, and he was trying to talk to me and drive down River Road in that storm."

"You were on the phone with him when he crashed." Gage wasn't asking, but Nanette tearfully nodded.

He pulled her into his arms and held her. "Oh, Nanette, I'm so sorry."

"What if I killed him, Gage?" *And what if I loved him?*

"He hasn't given up yet, Nan, and even if it is his time to cross, you know as well as I do that there's nothing anyone on this side can do to change it. The powers that be will determine whether he's meant to stay here longer."

She swallowed, sniffed. "I want to see him."

He tightened his hold on her. "Nanette, CCU is only open to visitors twice a day, and then only two family members at a time. Family members, Nanette."

She leaned away from him, blinking the tears from her eyes. "Gage, I have to see him. I *have* to."

"The only way I can let you go back is if Roussel's family says it's okay. The unit opens at eight in the morning for guests and is only open for an hour. Same thing at eight tomorrow night, and that's it."

"Surely they'll let me," Nanette said, refusing to think otherwise. She had been the one who'd found him on the road, hadn't she? And they didn't know that she was the reason he'd been there in the first place.

"I'll ask Johnny in the morning. He said he'd be here before the doors open." Gage paused. "If Charles gets worse, we may not let anyone in, Nan. We don't want family members to come in overly upset and disturb Charles while his body is trying to heal. He may not be conscious, but I'm a firm believer that those hovering on the brink can hear and feel everything around them. I'm not going to risk his family upsetting him now, and I won't risk you upsetting him, either."

"I'd never do that."

"I don't mean with anger, Nan—I know you better than that. I mean you apologizing for putting him where he is, or something along that line. It isn't your fault, anyway, but he damn sure doesn't need to hear you say it is."

"I wouldn't." She just wanted to see him, touch him…let him know that she cared.

"I'll ask Johnny first thing in the morning."

"I'll be here."

Gage sighed. "There's a strong chance Johnny may not let you see his brother, Nanette. There's no reason for you to drive all the way back over here in the morning just to have to go back home. Why don't you let me talk to him first, then if Johnny says it's okay, you can come during tomorrow night's visit."

"I'm not leaving. I'll be here until the morning visiting hour, and then again at the evening one, if necessary. Johnny will let me go back. And Charles will make it through this. He has to."

"Nan, there's a good chance that *no one* will get to see him in the morning. Just go home, and let me call you and give you his status in the morning."

"No."

"What about school? Your class?" Gage questioned her.

"You said CCU is open an hour, right?" When he nodded, she continued, "I'll get a substitute teacher for the first block and go in late."

"You hate getting substitutes," Gage said, "and you still don't know if you'll be able to see him, Nanette. I really think you should wait until tomorrow night, if he even—"

"Don't say it," she warned, not wanting to hear him say that Charles might not be here tomorrow night.

"I wasn't going to say that. I was talking about Johnny. I was about to say *if* Johnny even allows you to go back and see him."

"He will. I'll make sure of it, somehow."

But after six hours of sitting and half dozing on the uncomfortable couch, Nanette realized that it didn't matter whether Johnny Roussel approved her entry to the CCU. Gage, along with the other doctors assigned to Charles, vetoed visitations altogether.

"His condition isn't worse, but it isn't better, either," Gage said, "and we don't want to risk upsetting him right now. We'll do our best to provide visitation this evening."

Nanette stood alongside Charles's family for the disheartening news. Then she told them and Gage that she'd be back in the evening and left to head toward school—to return to her life while, because of her, Charles Roussel barely clung to his.

5

THE LIGHT WAS BLINDING. Charles had seen a light nearly this vivid only a few times before, when he was driving home in the late afternoon and the potent Louisiana sun burned his eyes as it fought its setting over the bayou before fading into night. But even on those rare occasions, it wasn't this bright. And unlike those times, this burst of illumination didn't cause him to squint or reach for sunglasses; quite the opposite, his eyes didn't seem to mind the glow at all, nor did the rest of his body, drawn to the warmth, the beauty, of the all-encompassing light.

He stepped toward it, relished the undeniable feeling of euphoria that seemed to reach toward him, beckoning him to come closer, to forget everything else but what hid within that flame.

Charles wondered whether this was a dream. Could a dream feel so amazing? So wonderful? So right? Cause him to feel such peace? He'd never experienced anything like this while asleep before. Typically, his dreams were cluttered with deadlines and goals for the parish, ways to work the political system to achieve what he wanted, family drama and the problems of his past. Whenever he *could* make it beyond those obstacles, he had dreams of hot and steamy sex with the most exquisite black-haired Cajun beauty.

He paused his progress toward the light, recalling the woman who had reigned over those fantasies for the past twelve years. What was it about her now, about Nanette, that made him want to turn away from the magical lure of the light? It felt good moving closer, but it also felt…wrong. As though this wasn't the way he should be going after all, and if he followed through then he'd never have another vision of the two of them, writhing in sexual fervor like crazed sex-starved teens. The way they had the first time in that erotic house of mirrors.

The light was tempting. Extremely tempting. But not *that* tempting.

Why did that welcoming light seem to be both the beginning of something new and an ending? An ending to something he'd never completed, with Nanette.

The analytical part of him began forcing facts together, pushing the puzzle pieces up front and center. As long as he looked at the light, he couldn't remember details, couldn't place how this dream had begun.

So he turned away, and the heat of the light grew even more potent, singeing his back, as though he were making the wrong decision.

Was he?

Nanette. The one thought that made him question whether he should continue this dream at all was Nanette. But this dream wasn't even about her, and try as he might, he couldn't bring her into it, which seemed somewhat odd, since this was *his* dream.

Charles thought about that, and tried to recall what he'd been doing before he went to sleep. Strangely enough, he couldn't remember going to bed. Couldn't even remember arriving home after work.

He closed his eyes and took another step away from the light. The searing heat on his back lessened. He took another step, and another then immediately heard rain. He couldn't see any water; his surroundings were too foggy. Everything that wasn't enclosed in the light seemed virtually nonexistent. But as he continued to move farther away from its illumination and allowed himself to go deeper into the fog, then he recalled what had happened.

Rain. He'd actually seen the storm ahead of him on River Road, that wet wall progressing down the Mississippi on a direct collision course with his path.

Cindy's call. His niece had called and apologized for giving out his cell number, and Charles had told her to be careful, not to venture on River Road until the storm had passed. He'd been worried she might have an accident.

Accident. He'd been on the phone, but he was no longer talking to Cindy. Nanette had called, and she was angry. No, not angry—hurt. He'd hurt her, and that had bothered him immensely. He'd promised to rectify things, to correct the wrong he'd done to her and to her family when he met with the historical society, but she hadn't believed him. She was too hurt, too upset, and Charles had been trying to calm her down when that shadow, that dog, came out of nowhere. Then he'd swerved, and he'd heard her screams.

"Mon Dieu, I'm dead." He whirled to view the light again and realized that he'd continued moving away from it as he'd flashed through his memories of that drive home and the conversation with Nanette.

He *couldn't* lose his life now. If he was dead, then he'd

have no chance to follow through on his promise to her, no chance to tell the historical society that he'd been wrong, and that her house should stand. If he was dead, he'd have no chance to be with her again. Ever.

Charles moved his feet faster, determined to get as far away from the light as possible. The dead were supposed to go to the light, right? So if he moved away, maybe, just maybe, he could stay closer toward the living. Maybe he could stay closer to her, long enough to somehow find a way to tell her that he was sorry, that he hadn't meant to hurt her, hadn't meant to hurt her family. What if, because of his stupid attempts to stay closer to her via their ongoing fight, he caused her to lose what she loved the most, that home?

"I'm not going anywhere near that light until I see her." He yelled the words, not knowing whether anyone would hear, or care. But in the distance, a thundering rumble resonated, and within seconds, he felt the vibrations from its force against his feet. He moved faster, but his legs were heavy, as though running through water. "I'm not," he said resolutely. And he prayed that he had the power, the will, to follow through with that promise. Could he keep himself away from the light? *Could* he find a way to let Nanette know that he did care? That he hadn't meant to hurt her?

Charles didn't know, but he wasn't going to succumb to the pull of the light until one way or another, he found out.

He tried to run faster and found that the farther he was from the light, the more tired he became. He stopped, clutching his chest as a sensation that seemed mighty close to what he'd expect during a heart attack bore down on his entire being. Was he being punished for not going into the light like a good little dead man? He smirked at that. Leave it to a lawyer to test the rules of heaven and hell.

He closed his eyes, waited until the pain subsided a bit, then concentrated. He'd handle this the way he handled any other problem, with a well-orchestrated plan. Problem was, he was clueless about how this all worked. How many options did a dead guy have? And was there any way to change the terms? He shook his head. He was dead, and still strategizing. In any case, he was ready to negotiate with whoever was listening.

"I need to fix it, to take care of what I've done to the Vicknair family, and to Nanette, before I go over," he said, and it was much harder to talk this time. His words pushed out as though he'd just finished a triathlon and didn't have the breath for speech. But he wasn't giving up. He *wasn't* going to that light until he corrected his mistake.

"Help me fix it, and then—then I'll think about walking through." He didn't know whether this appeal would work with whoever was listening or not, since he honestly wasn't sure whether they could force him into the light if they really wanted. As weak as he felt right now, he rather suspected they could.

Have mercy, it hurt to realize that this was it. He'd never completed his political goals, never found himself in the governor's mansion, or hell, the White House. More than that, he hadn't even had kids, no one to carry on his name— and he'd never truly experienced love.

It really bit to die young.

"Come on," he continued. "She'll lose her house, and I can't bear that for the rest of—eternity. Don't make me."

Immediately, the fog in front of him thinned, and the

pain in his chest lessened again. Charles moved forward to find himself before a door he recognized. He was at the St. Charles Parish Courthouse, and the door ahead of him led to the council chambers, where the historical society met. Charles heard voices inside the room and wondered who was meeting there now.

No sooner did he have the thought than he found himself on the other side, in the council chambers. As usual, the long black table that centered the room was surrounded by members of the River Road Historical Society. The only thing that wasn't usual was the man at the head of the table, in the seat designated for the chair of the committee—Charles. Now Paul Remondet, the second most vocal society member, next to Charles, sat in the prominent black leather chair at the table.

Charles felt a mild ping of disappointment at seeing how quickly they'd moved on, with Paul filling his space as though it didn't matter that Charles wasn't there.

Wait a minute. The society meeting was scheduled for Tuesday. But today was Monday. Charles shook his head. Hell, he'd lost a day already. Obviously, time flew when you were dead.

But he wasn't even all that cold yet, and they'd gone on with the meeting without him. Wasn't there some sort of memorial service they should be attending? Or perhaps at least postponing the meeting until their parish president was laid to rest? Talk about your lack of sympathy.

Charles snarled at Paul, then added a growl for good measure, and the guy didn't so much as flinch. Perfect, he was a ghost with no ability to haunt. Where was the fun in that?

Remondet cleared his throat and rapped a wooden

gavel—Charles's wooden gavel—against the table, and the chatter in the room died down.

"For those of you who I haven't spoken to personally today, I want to remind you that I am in no way trying to take the place of our committee head. I'm only filling in for President Roussel until he recovers."

Charles blinked. *Recovers?*

"Have you heard anything else about his condition?" Julia Marousek asked from the far end of the table, while Charles placed his hand to his chest. He couldn't *feel* his heart beating. And if it was, how was he here?

"I went to the hospital, but they weren't allowing anyone to go back and see Charles. He's still in CCU, and apparently they're even keeping the family away until they're certain he's stable enough to handle visitors. As of tonight, that hasn't happened. And I have to say that his family has really been through the mill over the past twenty-four hours."

A collective round of "bless their hearts" was mumbled from the female members of the society, while the men all merely shook their heads at his dire condition.

Dire, Charles repeated. Not dead.

But if he wasn't dead, then what was he, exactly?

Before he had a chance to figure that one out, Paul continued. "As we know, President Roussel was completely onboard with our latest decision to move up the final inspections of homes applying for society funding, and that's the main reason I decided that we should go ahead and hold tonight's meeting. Charles would have wanted us to continue our progress, and I don't want to disappoint him when he returns by falling down on the job. Now, the letters should have arrived at all homes for which funding has been requested, so they will anticipate our final inspection on the first of September." Paul frowned, then added, "Just so you know, I did see one of the River Road plantation owners tonight at the hospital, oddly enough. Nanette Vicknair."

"She was there to see President Roussel?" Wendy Millwood asked. "But I thought the woman hated him. I mean, that's the indication I got every time we went there for an inspection."

"From what I was told, Ms. Vicknair was the first to arrive on the scene of President Roussel's accident."

Nanette had been the first on the scene? How was that possible? She'd been talking to Charles when he'd wrecked. Had she heard the collision? Well, of course she had, and then she'd gone looking for him, in spite of the fact that he'd been a horse's ass to her for the past three years.

Paul cleared his throat. "We didn't speak of the society's decisions, of course, since we both were there because of President Roussel's tragic accident. However, I have no doubt that we will hear from her again when we make our final decisions, unless those recommendations veer away from the direction we've anticipated."

"That the Vicknair home, as well as the other ten on the bottom half of our list, shouldn't receive restoration funding?" Eddie Solomon asked. Eddie was the oldest member of the committee and rarely spoke, so when he did, everyone listened. "A shame, considering how long the family has been a dominant presence in the parish."

"That's true," Charles said, leaning toward Eddie so the man could hear. "Tell them that it should be saved, Solomon. Come on. Give them your opinion. I know you don't think we should tear that place down."

Eddie's weathered face shifted with his frown. "I'd planned to discuss the Vicknair plantation further at tonight's meeting, ask Charles why he felt so strongly about the place. But with his accident and all, that isn't possible." His wiry white brows quirked downward to join the frown. "Can't say that I'm willing to speak against his recommendation now, though, all things considered. Yeah, I suppose that one will remain on the bottom half of the list, unless by some miracle the family provides a reason to bump it up." He rolled his lips inward as he apparently thought about what he was going to say, then he added, "President Roussel was right. The place can't withstand another storm without some major work. It'd take a large portion of our funds, and it's probably best to use our money on saving more places that are worthy of it."

"It is worthy of it!" Charles yelled, raising his voice in vain. No one could hear.

What had he done?

"I do love the way it looks from the street, though," Wendy said wistfully. "There's nothing like a big old sugarcane plantation. Adds to the appeal of the parish, in my opinion."

"But what kind of appeal will it have if it gets hit with another hurricane?" Paul asked. "The bottom floor was filled with sludge and flood water, and I'm sure it probably surpassed the National Association of Home Builders' guidelines for demolition. If we'd have gotten out there in time to measure, I have no doubt we'd have found the lowest floor stood more than six feet in floodwater. And if we'd had proof of that, the place would've already been destroyed."

"But we didn't get proof," Julia pointed out. "And several of the places on the top half of our list were also probably beyond the NAHB's guidelines."

Eddie Solomon nodded. "True, but President Roussel firmly stated that the Vicknair place shouldn't receive funding, and I believe, particularly now, that we should respect the parish president's wishes."

"I have to agree," Paul said from the head of the table. "Unless, by some miracle, the Vicknair place lands National Register status before the final inspection, then I'm going to keep it where it is on the funding list, in the lower half."

Charles's head reeled with the surplus of information he'd gained. One, he wasn't dead, but he wasn't in the best of shape, either. Two, they were continuing progress toward an early inspection, which wasn't a problem, as long as the Vicknair place got moved to the top half of the list, which it wouldn't, because of him. Damn it. And three, Nanette had gone looking for him, found him, then had gone to the hospital. To see him.

Of the three points of interest, that one topped the lot.

While the historical society continued discussing the other homes on their list, Charles left the room. So, he wasn't dead, but he wasn't much alive at the moment, either. Still, he had no doubt that what he'd just witnessed in that room had really happened. Somehow, he'd managed to mentally observe their meeting, while his body recovered—damn, he hoped he was recovering—at the hospital.

So, deductive reasoning would lead him to believe…if he could get to the historical society meeting, then he could probably get to other places, too.

And right now, he knew exactly where he wanted to be.

6

NANETTE WAS SO TENSE that she wasn't certain whether trying to sleep would do a bit of good. But she had to teach in the morning, and God knew she needed some rest in order to pull that off. She set her alarm, because if she did manage to go to sleep, there was no telling if she'd wake up on her own.

What day was it, anyway? She struggled to work her way back through time. Sunday she'd been up most of the night dreaming of Charles. Monday was the first day of school, and she'd come home to find that letter and make that doomed telephone call. Then came the horrible crash, and she'd spent the night—last night—at the hospital. Today she'd tried to see him, both at the morning visitation and again at the evening one, but Gage and the other doctors hadn't budged on letting anyone in. So she and Charles's family had finally returned to their respective homes.

So what day was it, again?

Sitting on the edge of the bed, Nan rubbed her forehead with her fingers and concentrated. Tuesday. Today was Tuesday.

Had it really only been one day since Charles's wreck?

She glanced back at the alarm clock. Had she set it, or not? She pressed the wake button, saw that it was set, then dropped to the bed. She hadn't taken the time to put on sleep clothes, and she wasn't going to leave the bed now that she was here, so she wiggled out of her pants, tossed her T-shirt to the floor, then climbed under the covers in her bra and panties.

Exhaustion, both physical and emotional, saturated her body, yet her eyes wouldn't close. Instead, they focused on the poster she'd purchased the day after her first time with Charles. She'd had to have it.

Nan turned her head on the pillow and forced her attention to the window on the opposite wall, where a sliver of a moon was centered in the jet-black sky. There were no stars around the skinny crescent; there was nothing but bleak darkness. The moon was simply there, by itself in the dark, completely alone. Like her.

Perhaps it was because she'd been waiting to see him all day, or maybe it was because he always dominated her dreams at night, but in no time at all, images of Charles Roussel filled her thoughts, and these images didn't have anything to do with hospitals or car crashes or telephone calls. They had everything to do with desire, her desire for the boy she'd loved so long ago—and the man she still wanted more than anything.

Nanette rolled onto her back and pushed the covers to the floor, then slid her palms down her abdomen toward her panties and thought of Charles, the way he'd looked the last time she saw him, with his eyes all smoky and incredibly sexy, and that wicked devil's dimple teasing her with his smile just before he'd kissed her. In her mind they were outside of the plantation, and she was backed against his car, with his muscular body moving closer. She'd felt so helpless against the pull of him, but the truth was—she hadn't wanted help. She'd only wanted him.

"Please," she whispered, and her fingertips edged beneath the lacy underwear.

The room grew warmer, almost electric with a sensation that was oddly familiar. Her hands stilled momentarily, and she slowly opened her eyes. Charles stood near the bed, his eyes as dark and hazy as ever, and filled with unhidden desire.

Nanette knew this wasn't real. His image was perfect, the way it'd been before the crash. No slash marred the left side of his face. In fact, he had no sign of any physical ailment. But even though it was only a dream, she wanted him more than ever, and if having him in her dreams was the only way to make that happen, then she'd take it.

"Please," she whispered, and she slid her panties down her legs and pushed them to the floor.

Dream Charles stepped closer to the bed, and his attention moved to her center, bare and ready and pulsing...for him.

"Please," she repeated, knowing that this dream was hers to control, but still wanting it to seem Charles's decision to take her, want her, the way she wanted him.

She rose slightly, unclasped her bra and removed it, then tossed it to the floor. Her hips lifted, and her hands fisted in the bedding as she fought to keep from touching her sensitive folds. It'd be so easy to bring herself to climax now, but she wanted to let the dream prevail, to at least have the semblance of Charles Roussel bringing her to orgasm. Her fingernails clawed the mattress as she looked at him and pleaded again.

"I need you."

Nanette almost wept with joy when he removed his clothes. Definitely nothing physically wrong with the Charles in her dream. He was even more chiseled than she remembered. More masculine than the young man he'd been when she was eighteen. More defined. More mesmerizing. She licked her lips and studied the thick, prominent erection standing boldly against his abdomen.

Her core burned to feel him inside, deep inside, and Nanette realized that she'd never had a more detailed dream, one that seemed so amazingly real. She barely comprehended a scratching noise overpowering the room, before finally becoming aware that it was her nails digging into the mattress while he moved onto the bed.

She whimpered, almost sure that she actually felt the heat of him touching her skin. He lay on his side and gently brushed her tears away as he eased his fingers through her hair, then brought a dark lock to his lips and kissed it.

Nanette quivered, wanting those lips to kiss all of her with such tenderness. The dream Charles obviously knew what she wanted, because his face lowered to hers, and those magical lips pressed against her own, probing them to open to his perusal. His tongue, hot and wet, swept inside, and Nanette moaned against the sweet invasion. While the kiss continued, she sensed his hands cupping her breasts and kneading them sensually, while her hips moved in a building rhythm, and her center grew hotter, wetter.

He growled appreciatively, and Nanette was extremely impressed that her dream allowed her not only to hear the intensity of that growl, but also to feel the vibration against her mouth. She clutched the mattress more fiercely, until her hands became numb, and twisted her hips to press her wet core against his thigh. Then she turned her head to briefly break the kiss and gasped, "Inside me, please!"

Another low, throaty growl erupted from him, and he shifted all of his weight on top of her, using his powerful thigh to push her legs apart, then pressed the thick tip of his erection against her hot opening.

Throwing her head back, Nanette pushed her legs wider and shoved her hips upward as she fought to have what was so deliciously close.

His hands moved to her hips and he grasped them so tightly she winced, then he shoved his entire length inside.

Nanette's intimate walls struggled to accept the breadth of his penis. His forceful grunts resonated throughout her room as he thrust into her again and again, and the spiraling tension inside of her built to a feverish pitch. Her body hovered on the brink of a climax that she so desperately needed.

"Charles!" she screamed, her cries in time with each commanding stroke, and stars burst behind her lids, then the rush of her release boiled through her, her inner muscles rippling around the flesh within her. His yell of fulfillment roared free as he climaxed deep inside her.

Nanette waited for her postorgasmic shudders to settle, then she slowly opened her eyes. Her hands still clutched the mattress as if her life depended on it, and she eased her cramped fingers open, then wiggled them, wincing at the painful tingle of blood passing back through.

Never had she had an orgasm so powerful in a dream. Never had she experienced a dream that felt so real. She moved her hand to her belly and downward, where she could swear she still felt the blissful sensation of a man's touch—or Charles Roussel's touch—deep within her. She hadn't even touched herself, yet she'd climaxed harder than ever before. It'd seemed as though it was Charles himself bringing her to the most erotic orgasm of her life.

Her eyes burned, then her tears pushed free. That was what she wanted more than anything, another chance to be with him, to give herself to him, the way she did in her dreams.

"Please," she whispered to the ceiling. "If you can help me at all—if you can help him at all—give me another chance."

7

THE LIGHT WAS SCALDING HOT and beckoning. Crumpled on the floor, Charles woke to find his cheek flush against the cool surface and his body shivering uncontrollably. He was drained, completely and totally. No energy to stand. No energy to speak. Moving closer to that light would help; he knew it as certainly as he knew his name.

He grappled at the floor, and slid his heavy body farther away from its warmth. He couldn't go to the light, no matter how much he knew it'd help the pain in his body, in his head, in his heart. Going into that light meant going away from Nanette.

And he damn well wasn't leaving her now.

She wanted him. Not just any man, but *him*.

Earlier, when he'd found himself in that room with the historical society, Charles had known that it wasn't a dream. Somehow, his spirit had left his body at the hospital and made its way to that room, seen what had transpired between those committee members. And when he'd found his way to Nanette Vicknair's bedroom, that'd been real, too. As real as the lovemaking they'd just shared.

He still couldn't fathom how he'd ended up in her bedroom, no more than he understood how he'd ended up in that meeting. He'd simply thought about where he wanted to be, and there he was.

He'd never in his life become so hard so fast as when he'd entered that room to find Nan on the bed wearing nothing but a skimpy black bra and panties. Her breasts had practically spilled over the lacy cups of that bra, and with the way her breath came out ragged as she moved her hands toward the sexy panties, they wouldn't have been contained long.

Charles swallowed thickly. She'd looked at him, then removed the panties and bra, while he'd forced himself to merely watch. He'd never seen anything as sexy, as erotic, as Nanette Vicknair, aroused and eager to come. He'd fought for composure, for restraint and for the ability to remain in that room without doing anything stupid that would cause him to leave. He didn't know the rules to this spirit travel thing, and he sure didn't want to break them when he was finally near her, watching her, wanting her.

When she'd opened her eyes and looked at him, begged him to come closer, Charles couldn't believe it. And when she'd coaxed him to her bed, and against her naked, sexually heated body, he'd thought that surely he was dead. Because he didn't think he'd ever felt anything closer to heaven.

Then he'd made love to her, and he'd known. There was nothing better. Ever. He had no idea how it was possible, but it'd been real. And glorious.

Charles realized that Nanette, in bed and obviously aroused before he'd even entered the room, had probably thought she was dreaming. And for a moment, he'd considered not taking advantage of that, not giving in to the male urge to give her exactly what she wanted without thought that she may not want it from him.

Then she'd said his name. And Charles had nearly come merely from hearing it on her lips. Her dream, her fantasy, was about him.

His body may feel like hell now, but regardless, his dick was hardening again. He wanted her again. He'd gotten to her before by merely thinking of her.

Charles shut his eyes, thought of Nanette.

He opened them to find himself still flush against the floor and still feeling as though he'd been through hell. Literally.

The light seemed to blaze a little brighter, and the warmth of it did feel incredibly good against his shivering skin. But Charles wasn't stupid. The light might feel good, but Nanette felt better, and he wasn't about to hand his soul over if there was the least chance that he could have what he wanted once more. Somehow he had to figure out how to find her again.

But first, unfortunately, he had to rest. Because at the moment, Charles felt drained, exhausted. He closed his eyes again, and found that no matter how hard he tried, this time he couldn't open them.

8

NANETTE ENTERED THE PLANTATION Thursday afternoon to find Monique, Chantelle, Jenee and Celeste gathered around the kitchen table. She'd seen all of the family cars outside so she'd known they were here, but she had no idea why. And she was too tired to try to put it together. Between the hours at the hospital, the hours at school and the hours of dreaming about Charles, there wasn't a lot of time left for sleep.

Then again, she hadn't dreamed about him last night, which was odd, given she'd actually tried to. She'd desperately wanted to connect with him in her mind, since she couldn't see him in person. On Wednesday morning, when Johnny Roussel, the remainder of Charles's family and Nanette had shown up anticipating a visit, Gage had informed them that Charles's condition had actually weakened through the night, and they still couldn't allow visitors. Ditto for Wednesday night and this morning.

Would she at least get to dream about him tonight, the way she'd done Tuesday night? That dream, the passion of it, the desire, had overpowered her thoughts for the past two days. Sure, she'd fantasized about Charles often over the past decade, but never like this. How had she climaxed without the slightest touch? And why did she feel like she *had* been touched, deeper than she'd ever been touched before?

"Nanette? Are you okay?" Monique asked, standing from the table and moving toward the counter. "Let me get you something to drink. I know you've had a rough week."

Nanette still had a hard time getting used to seeing Monique's typically petite frame showcasing an extremely swollen belly. She cradled one hand under her stomach as she moved, ever protective of the child that'd be here within the next few weeks.

"You want some wine?" Monique continued.

Nanette shook her head. "Water, please." She didn't need anything that might make her the least bit light-headed. She'd be heading to the hospital soon to wait for the evening visit.

A loud noise, followed by the distinctive sound of Tristan cursing, echoed from the front of the house.

"What is he doing?" Nanette asked. "Actually, what are all of you doing here?"

"Gage told us about the change in the inspection date, and that you'd been spending every minute away from school at the hospital trying to see Roussel." Jenee's mouth dipped down at one side as she added, "That accident wasn't your fault, Nan."

"I really don't want to talk about it right now." Nanette accepted the glass of water from Monique and took a seat at the table. She'd been thinking about nothing but the accident, and the possibility that Charles might not recover for days, but she simply couldn't speak about it, even with her family.

Another loud "Damn it!" bellowed through the house, and Nan peered over her glass at the other Vicknair women at the table.

"Care to tell me what they're tackling in there, because it sounds like I don't want to see it."

"They're finishing up with the stairs, I think. And from what I've heard them yelling, I believe the nail gun has been jamming a bit." Celeste stood, crossed the kitchen and pushed the swinging door open to glance down the hall. "Yep, they're definitely working on the stairs, but I'm not about to ask if it's the nail gun still giving them trouble." She closed the door on the curses and hammering and returned to the table. "Well, except for Ryan and his ghosts. I believe they're in the attic, but I'm not sure what they're working on."

"Ghosts?" Nan asked.

"I think Grandma Adeline's looking out for us. That construction guy, the one who finished the crown molding in the front room, crossed after the job was done," Monique explained, taking over the conversation about her husband. "But today, he got two more ghosts that want to leave their mark before they cross over. Evidently, a lot of guys who build things want to make sure there's something lasting that they created left on this side when they go." She nodded, looking thoughtful as she spoke. "I can see Ryan being that way, wanting to make sure that he's left something behind for others to admire. I think it'd be a sense of pride to a construction worker, don't you think?"

"Makes sense to me," Chantelle agreed.

"Anyway," Monique continued, "after Gage called from the hospital and told us about the deadline getting moved up, we all decided that we'd try to rearrange our work schedules as much as possible this week and next, so that the house will stand a chance in the inspection next Saturday. That is when they're coming, right?"

"The letter said on or before September 1, which is

actually on the following Monday, so I'd guess you're right. Not this weekend, but next," Nan said. Since Charles's accident, she hadn't given any thought to the inspection. It didn't seem to matter as much with his life in jeopardy.

"That's what we'll shoot for then," Jenee said. "A week from Saturday. I know we can't finish everything, but we'll give it our best shot." She shrugged. "That's all we can do, right?"

"And you can spend your time teaching and going to the hospital. We know that's what's on your mind now. Besides, you've always been the one spearheading the work on the house. Let us take control for a while, so you can check on Roussel." Kayla's words were so true that Nan's chest constricted with emotion. She *had* always put the house before anything else, until now. Now her priority was with Charles.

"Nan, we've noticed something before, but never really pushed you about it. Now, with everything happening, we're concerned for you, so I'm just going to ask," Monique stated softly. "You and Charles, it isn't merely the house issue, is it? I'll admit we've discussed it this afternoon, and we wonder if there isn't more between you two than you've admitted before."

Nanette had worked hard to keep her past with Charles where it belonged, in the past. As the oldest cousin, not to mention the oldest medium, she'd known from early on that she wanted to be a role model to the rest. She wanted to be seen as smart, wise enough to lead this generation of Vicknair mediums as they helped as many spirits as possible. Losing her virginity—and her heart— to a guy who'd left without looking back wasn't something she wanted to be known for. Neither was that fiery, impulsive nature that had put her in that situation to begin with. It was always there, lurking beneath the surface. Yet the only one who could still ignite that fire was Charles.

In her heated dealings with him about the house, the family had witnessed firsthand the obvious tension between them. And then there had been that kiss. Even so, Nanette had never discussed what happened between them with any of her cousins before, and she sure didn't want to start now.

"You don't have to tell us if you don't want to talk about it right now," Jenee said.

"I don't," Nanette said, then felt a stab of guilt at keeping them so in the dark, particularly when they were all willing to take over her quest to save the house and let her focus on Charles. She sighed. "But you're right. There is more to the two of us, and if he wakes up—" she winced "—I mean *when* he wakes up, and after we have a chance to discuss everything, then I'll tell you more."

All heads at the table nodded, as though Nanette's vague explanation sufficed. She was extremely grateful. "I'm going to change and then go to the hospital. I think there's some leftover gumbo in the fridge if you want something to eat."

"We can handle the cooking," Chantelle said. "Just leave things around here to us for a while. And when you come back down, I'll have a sandwich waiting for you. You can eat it on the way to the hospital."

"I'm not hungry."

"But you're going to eat anyway, to keep up your strength," Monique said, in a motherly tone that somehow seemed to suit her now that she was pregnant.

Nanette's tears welled, and she managed a smile. "I don't know what to say."

"A simple thanks will do," Jenee said.

"Thanks."

Two hours later, she arrived at the hospital waiting room with half a turkey sandwich and a bottle of water tucked in her teacher's tote, and the memory of her entire family, as well as a couple of ghosts she couldn't see, bidding her farewell as she left the plantation. Their kindness touched her more than she could express, and gave her the courage she needed to continue feeling positive toward Charles's recovery. Tonight, hopefully, Gage and the other doctors at the hospital would finally allow Charles's family, and Nanette, to see him.

She reached the CCU waiting room and noticed something was different from every other time she'd been there. For the first time, the Roussel family wasn't camped out on the orange vinyl seats. Instead, that same family was huddling just outside the CCU doors. Nanette's heart plunged to her stomach. This could be good or very bad.

"Please, let it be good," she breathed.

Nanette moved toward the group. She'd been talking with them daily in the waiting room, but she really wasn't all that familiar with any of the Roussels, except for Charles and Johnny. Charles because of their history, and Johnny because they were neighbors. Her relationship with Johnny wasn't the neighborly norm, either, since he knew *something* had transpired between her and his brother years ago. She'd actually asked him—once—if he thought Charles was ever coming back to Louisiana, and she'd seen the answer in his gray eyes, full of pity, even before he'd said what she hadn't wanted to hear—"No."

Now her main communication with the younger Roussel brother was primarily restricted to waving when they both happened to be outside their homes and idle chitchat if they happened to reach their respective mailboxes at the same time. And since that one awkward conversation so long ago, they'd never mentioned Charles. However, this week, she had talked more substantially with him, and they'd spoken nonstop of Charles, with Johnny discussing his brother's hopes and dreams, and the fact that all of those may very well be null and void now.

That thought had hurt Nanette more than she'd admit, and she wouldn't let her mind dwell too much on it now. He simply had to get better.

She wanted to talk to Johnny again, ask him what was going on, why the entire family stood by those doors anxiously peering at the tiny crack between them as though they could will them open. Unfortunately, Johnny wasn't part of the bunch. Which meant he was probably on the other side.

Because he was getting to see his brother? Or because he was learning that he'd never see him again?

Nanette fought the instant nausea that had her rethinking the half a turkey sandwich she'd eaten on the drive over. She swallowed and mustered her courage to ask what was happening, but before she had a chance to speak, the doors opened, and Johnny and Charles Senior stepped out.

"Daddy, can I see *Paran* now?" Cindy Roussel asked.

Johnny's mouth was grim as he said, "Cindy, he looks rough, not at all himself. He's got a bandage covering a good portion of his face, a lot of tubes all over, and his coloring isn't so good. I know you want to go in, *chère,* but I'm not sure you should right now."

"Please, Daddy. I have to see him."

Nanette watched as Charles Senior looked at his son and nodded, silently telling him that he should grant his daughter's request. Johnny's wife stepped forward, wrapped an arm around Cindy and said, "I'll go with her, honey."

Johnny reluctantly agreed, and Cindy and her mother moved past Gage, while Johnny turned back to Nanette's cousin and asked, "Is that normal? For him to look so…"

He stopped abruptly, but Charles Senior cleared his throat and added, "Dead. *Mon Dieu,* son, he looks dead. Is he—" He breathed in thickly through his mouth, then released it. "Is he going to die, Doctor? Is that why you let us go back tonight? So we could see him before he does?"

Nanette held her breath while she waited with the rest of Charles's family for Gage's answer. *Say no, Gage. Say no. Please.*

"Mr. Roussel, I know this is difficult to hear, and I wish I could give you a more definite answer. But the truth is, at this point, I can't make any promises." He paused to put a hand on the father's shoulder and continued, "But his condition has improved marginally since yesterday, and I did want you to be able to see him if at all possible. If seeing him as he is is too difficult, then—"

Charles Senior halted Gage's words, shaking his head and blinking through his tears. "No, no, son. I want to see Charles, whenever I can. It's just—just tough to take, you know. Please, let us see him as much as we can."

"I will." Gage glanced at Nanette, gave her a nod that

said he'd talk to her in a moment, then told the remainder of the family, "You can continue going back two at a time to visit over the next hour. If his condition is the same or hopefully improved by the time of the morning visit tomorrow, I'll let you back again."

"Thank you," Johnny said, moving to his father and slowly steering the older man toward the waiting room. "Come on, Pop, let me fix you some coffee."

Nanette quickly counted the remaining members of the Roussel family. She assumed they were cousins, aunts and uncles, but she didn't know any of them by name. There were nine total. If they went back in pairs, and if each stayed around ten minutes…there wouldn't be any time left for her to visit Charles. Her throat tightened.

"Nanette," Gage said, guiding her away from the group.

"How is he?" she asked, thinking the only way she may find out was from Gage, since it didn't appear she'd get to see Charles for herself. "Is it as bad as his daddy made it sound?"

"I'll tell you the truth, Nan. He's not in good shape, but compared to the way he was Wednesday morning, he's a hundred times better. I didn't know whether he'd make it through the day yesterday, but he did. And although he looks bad to his father and brother, in my opinion, something positive happened in the last twenty-four hours. He seems almost as though he's found strength. We're backing him off of the ventilator, and he's doing okay with that. That's a big step, and I told the Roussels that, but you can't blame them for being scared by his appearance. He does look bad, but medically speaking, he's improved. A lot."

Her relief was so powerful that her knees weakened, and

she leaned on Gage for support. He wrapped an arm around her and gently rubbed her back. "Listen, Nan. I can see you care about him. Hell, I've suspected it for years, and feel rather guilty that I never told you to get over whatever was holding you back and tell the guy how you feel. But now, when you get that chance, don't waste it. You wouldn't be practically living at this hospital if you didn't feel something incredibly strong for Roussel."

She nodded, too emotionally drained to argue or to attempt an explanation of the depth of her feelings for Charles, and the reasons she'd fought them for so long.

"Nanette." Johnny Roussel's voice caused them both to turn.

"Yes?"

"Do you still want to see him?"

She knew the rest of Charles's family hadn't been back yet, and apparently she didn't control her surprise that Johnny was asking if she wanted to go back before them, because he explained.

"You found him on that road, Nanette. We all know that, and we're grateful. And I know that the two of you were closer than anyone else realizes. Truthfully, I think if Charles could say something now, he'd tell me to let you go back. So, if you want to go on back…"

She looked at Gage, and he nodded toward the open door to CCU. "He's in room three."

"I'll try not to stay too long."

She passed through the doors and realized that she'd never been inside a Critical Care Unit before. It wasn't what she'd expected, though she didn't know exactly what she'd expected to see. A large circular nurses' station was centered in an open area, with a dozen or so rooms with curtained closures branching off in all directions. A series of beeps, some barely audible and others ear-piercing, echoed from beyond the thick curtains, and Nanette heard nurses communicating softly both within the curtained rooms and at the nurses' station.

Each room was identified by a large green number attached to the wall nearby, and Nanette gravitated toward one marked 3. A slight crack in the curtain showed the end of a bed, and a white sheet covering Charles's lower body. Gathering her strength, Nanette pushed the curtain open, stepped inside, and couldn't control the gasp that automatically escaped when she saw him.

Tubes. There were tubes everywhere, his nose, his mouth, his hand. Two large machines overpowered both sides of the bed, red and green lights flashing and numbers blinking steadily with each of Charles's forced breaths.

Nanette sat on a small stool next to the bed and, holding back her tears, she gently slid her upturned hand beneath Charles's. "I am so sorry," she whispered, looking at his bruised face as she spoke. The left side of his face, the area that she'd seen split open at the crash site, was bandaged completely, starting beside his eye and traveling down beneath his jaw. The right eye was dark purple and swollen, and his cheek was pale brown, or perhaps a grotesque combination of purple and yellow. His lips were slack and almost colorless, with a large tube passing through them, apparently traveling down his throat to allow him to breathe.

Another small gasp escaped before Nanette could get her emotions under control, and she attempted to swallow it away. He didn't need her sitting by his bed and whimpering. He needed strength. Gage had said that Charles appeared better today, and she wasn't about to mess that up. She wanted him to know that she was here, and that she'd be here for him if—no, *when*—he woke.

"Charles, it's Nanette. I've—I've been here every day since the accident, and I'm going to keep coming until you're better." She glanced toward the curtain, then back at him, leaning closer to whisper, "And when you are better, Charles, I want to try again. With us, I mean. I don't hate you. I tried to hate you for years, but I never did, not really." She smiled slightly. "Even when you were making me so angry I couldn't see straight I still wanted you. I still do." She eased off the chair and brushed a whisper-soft kiss against his forehead. "Charles, you can't leave yet. We've got unfinished business, you and I."

Nanette returned to her chair and looked at him, comparing the man before her to the one that she'd seen so clearly two nights ago in her mind. The image had been so perfect, Charles giving her…everything she wanted. Her heart hitched at the memory. He'd looked so incredibly alive, so incredibly sexy, all masculine and powerful and desirable…. That smoky gaze had studied her as he'd moved in to kiss her, and she'd literally been entranced by those eyes. Unable to look away. And his body—she glanced at the body now hidden beneath the sheets and at all of the tubes passing through this beautiful man—his body in her dream hadn't been through an accident.

If she hadn't called him while he was on that road, then he'd still look as healthy as he had in that dream. Beautifully vibrant, muscled and toned, all of him the picture of perfection, as he stood by her bed, practically beaming…

Nanette straightened on the stool, blinked at the man in the bed, and struggled to focus on what had finally clicked into place about that dream. She'd known something had seemed different, more realistic, about that dream than all her other ones. And now, finally, she realized what that was.

Charles Roussel had been beaming. Or, more precisely, glowing. The same way every ghost who visited her glowed.

This time, Nanette's gasp wasn't because of sadness; it was from sheer shock. "You—*mon Dieu*—you really *were* there Tuesday night."

The rings at the top of the curtain slid against the metal rod as Gage entered the enclosure with two of Charles's family members directly behind him. "Nanette, we need to let more of the family in, if they're all going to see Charles before visiting hours end."

Nanette realized that her hand was still beneath his, and she waited a heartbeat before sliding it free. *Squeeze it, Charles. Let me know that you know I'm here.*

Nothing happened. She slowly moved her palm across the sheet, then stood, nodding at the man and woman standing by her cousin before she stepped out of Charles's room and into the open CCU area, her mind spinning at the realization of what had truly happened Tuesday night.

Charles Roussel had been drifting between this life and the next, and instead of crossing over, he'd come to her. He'd visited her as a ghost. Her mind raced back to Tuesday night, and the way her hands had clenched the sheets. She hadn't touched him, not once. Throughout their entire lovemaking, she hadn't touched him. If she had, then she'd have broken one of the rules: the Vicknair mediums weren't allowed to touch spirits. Had she subconsciously known that Charles really was there? And that he was a ghost, so she shouldn't touch?

Had he known what he was doing? What they were doing? Or did he merely think he was dreaming, too? Because now she realized that what she'd suspected two weeks ago, when Charles had kissed her beside his car, was true. Charles Roussel wanted her. Almost as much as she wanted him.

She didn't wait to tell Gage goodbye, but walked mechanically through the hospital, her mind not really paying attention to anything around her as she left the building, climbed in her car and drove home.

Home to where, if dreams really did come true, she'd see Charles again. Soon.

9

CHARLES FELT AS THOUGH he was traveling River Road in the early morning, the fog from the Mississippi nearly drowning out all daylight but that powerful Louisiana sun still doing its best to shine through. That was what this was like, this stage in between life and death. He could see the light, as brilliant as it'd been last time, lurking ahead, but he wasn't moving closer. Instead, he remained in the thick fog, even though the light held the promise of no pain, no fear. That didn't matter. Somewhere within this fog, he'd find Nanette.

Charles concentrated on getting to her. He'd tried several times to make his way back, but had been unsuccessful. However, Charles Roussel had never been a quitter, and he sure as hell wasn't starting now. Their one heated encounter had haunted him throughout his journey through this seemingly endless fog, and he wasn't about to succumb to the light until he held her again.

"Come on, show me where she is." It felt like an eternity had passed since he'd been with her in her bedroom. And it could have—how would he know? Time was negligible here, and that wasn't a good thing. Last time, he'd lost a day before finding that meeting room and then Nanette. How many days had he lost this time?

"Nanette, I need you."

Squinting through the haze, he noticed an area where the mist wasn't quite so thick. He walked toward it, and within moments, he stood exactly where he wanted, in Nanette's room. *"Mon Dieu, I made it."* Gratitude to whatever forces had allowed him to find his way back filled his very being, and at the sight of her, a powerful yearning like he'd never experienced filled his soul. He wanted her, needed her and prayed he wouldn't have to leave anytime soon.

He was momentarily struck by the sweet sounds she made in her sleep. A deep thrum, almost purring, softly echoed with each breath. He could see her clearly, the light of the moon shining through the elongated window to spotlight the exquisite woman on the bed.

Her mouth was partially opened, black lashes fanned over the top of her cheeks, and long, silky jet-black hair tumbled wildly across the pillow. One arm had escaped the sheet and had exposed the sheer lacy triangles of black fabric barely covering Nanette's full breasts. Her nipples were taut, and he could make out their rosy hue beneath the filmy fabric.

Charles instantly grew hard. *Ça alors,* no woman was more beautiful.

He wasn't sure whether he walked or drifted to the bed, but either way, he was suddenly right there. And it'd taken him so long to return to her—or it felt that way—that he wasn't about to second-guess what he was doing.

Charles moved even closer, leaning over Nanette and brushing one long black strand away from her face. She moaned and turned her head toward him, and he simply couldn't stop. "Oh, *chère*," he said, and brought his lips to hers.

Like last time, his kiss ignited the passion always lurking just beneath Nanette Vicknair's surface. That passion had intrigued him way back when and still compelled him now, when he should probably be leaving this world completely and going to that light. But how could he? Why would he? He finally had a chance to have Nanette, and he felt more alive than he'd ever felt before the accident.

Her tongue caressed his, body squirming beneath him as though she couldn't get close enough, and her heat penetrated his flesh—if it could be called that—literally making him burn for more.

The hard points of her nipples pressed against his chest, and Charles moved over her, aligning their bodies so that his rock-hard penis pushed against her sweet center. He needed to remove the sheet, remove her nightgown and give in to the desire that had driven them both before. A desire controlling them again.

He lifted his body enough to grasp the edge of the sheet, and eased it down her body. Then he nudged her hair out of the way and placed whisper-soft kisses along her jaw in a path toward her ear. He gently pulled the lobe between his lips, then kissed her neck while she sucked in an excited breath.

"Let me love you, *chère. Mon Dieu,* I thought I wouldn't make it back to you."

Nanette jerked beneath him, and Charles knew he'd made a grave mistake. Last time, she'd undoubtedly thought she'd been dreaming. But this time, she was most definitely if slowly, waking up. And she seemed to know that someone was there. She could feel him—he knew that from her response to his touch. But she couldn't see him, and if she realized she was awake, would it terrorize her for him to touch her now?

He couldn't bear the thought of scaring her, so he eased up off the bed and moved away from the woman he wanted so much. What to do now? Did he merely think of leaving, and then let himself be whisked away? Or did he stay, and try to become a part of her dreams again, when she returned to sleep? And what kind of man would do that? Take advantage of a sleeping woman?

Charles knew exactly what kind of man. The kind who always believed the end result justified whatever it took to get there. The kind of man who'd use a woman's love for her home and her fear of losing it to be near her. The kind who thought he might not be hanging out in the land of the living much longer and finally had a chance to have the woman he wanted once more before he left. Charles wasn't always proud of the methods he used to get what he wanted, but whether he was proud of them or not, they worked. And right now, he wanted Nanette.

She had wanted him, too. She'd called out his name. *His* name. And oddly enough, though Charles was certain she couldn't see him, she was now fully awake and staring directly at him with hunger in her eyes.

Directly. At. Him.

Charles swallowed. *Could* she see him? Even when she wasn't in a dream state?

"Nanette," he said softly.

Her green eyes instantly filled with tears. "Charles," she whispered, her head shaking slightly as she said his name. "I—I thought you weren't coming back. I waited up all night last night, and you never came. Then Gage said that you were weaker, and I thought that I'd never have another chance to see you. I thought you'd crossed over. I'm—" her head continued to shake "—I'm so sorry."

Charles didn't know what to say. Not only could she see him, she could hear him, as well. He moved toward a chair by the bed and dropped into it, an onslaught of emotions hitting him like a hurricane bearing down on the levee. Questions mangled his thoughts. How could she see him? How could she hear him? And why didn't she look shocked at all? On the contrary, she'd said she'd waited up for him all last night, so she had *expected* him to come.

Charles didn't know what to ask first, so he decided to start with the basic information he was missing, and then work his way up to the rest. "What day is it?"

"Friday night," she whispered, scooting up onto the bed as she spoke. Charles had last been with Nanette on Tuesday, so he'd lost three more days. It'd taken *three days* to fight his way out of that fog and ignore the light and get back to her again.

Nanette's mouth trembled and she looked at Charles as though he were already dead. Which led him to his next question.

"How bad am I? I mean, the accident. How badly am I hurt? I am still alive, right?" He had to be. The guys at the historical society meeting had said he was in the CCU and that they thought he'd recover. And he'd been fighting the pull of that light for all he was worth. Surely he'd been successful, if he were here with Nanette.

"On Wednesday, your condition wasn't good, according to the doctors. But yesterday, you were better. They even let us see you. That's why I thought you'd come back here last night, but you didn't. And then Gage said your condition hadn't improved today, so I thought maybe you were getting ready to cross." She licked her lips, and Charles's cock twitched. He wanted her to help him figure out what was happening, since she obviously understood more about this than he did, but he also hated to waste his time with Nanette talking, particularly since they'd been on the verge of making love just a few moments ago, like they had Tuesday night.

And now that he realized she could see him, he also realized…

"You knew, didn't you? The other night, when I came here and was with you, you knew that it wasn't a dream."

She shook her head, and that delicate hollow between her breasts grew flushed. "When it happened, I thought I was dreaming. The way I always dream of you. Then I saw you at the hospital, and I realized that you'd really come to me."

The way I always dream of you. Though that was what he really wanted to address, there was something else he had to determine first.

"How did you know?" He leaned forward in the chair so that he was only a foot away from the bed.

"When I saw you in the hospital, you looked different than you had when you came to me." She hesitated, and Charles wondered what she wasn't saying. How bad had he looked at the hospital? Probably pretty damn bad, judging by the tenseness of her elegant jaw.

"Different how?" Exactly how many bones had he

broken? Or limbs had he lost? Hell, what exactly had happened after he'd hit the brakes?

"You weren't glowing."

Okay, not what he was expecting. "Glowing?"

"At the hospital, when I looked at your body, I knew that there was something different than when I'd seen you in my room. And then I realized that when you came to me the other night, you were glowing. You came to me as a ghost. And it was my fault. If I hadn't called you while you were driving in that storm, then you would've been paying more attention to the curves, and then you wouldn't have— wouldn't have—" A heart-wrenching sob tore from her, and that beautiful mouth trembled again as her tears made jagged paths down her face.

"Nanette, it wasn't your fault. I saw a dog run into the street ahead of me and I dodged it, but with the storm and the wet road and the curve, I lost control. You didn't cause the accident, *chère*."

She wiped more tears away, sniffed. "But if you hadn't been on the phone…"

"No," Charles said, halting her before she could continue. He would not let her take the blame for what had happened. "It wasn't your fault, and I don't want to hear you say it was. I was probably driving faster than I should, and I didn't have time to brake smoothly and miss that dog. That's what happened, and it would've happened regardless of whether I'd been on the phone with you at the time." Charles had to repeat himself several times, but eventually she seemed to finally believe that he was telling the truth; it wasn't her fault. Then he remembered the rest of what she'd said, that she'd known he was a ghost because he'd been glowing. *Glowing?*

He instinctively held out his hand and realized that he was, indeed, slightly shimmering. Why hadn't he noticed that before? Probably because he'd been so intent on getting back to Nanette that he hadn't spent any time taking stock of his own appearance.

"So you knew I was a ghost because I was glowing." A ghost, but not a dead ghost. Charles shook his head—nothing was making sense. If he was visible as a ghost, why hadn't the people at the historical society meeting seen him? He'd been mere inches away from Paul Remondet, and the guy hadn't so much as flinched. "But how did you see me the other night, Nanette? How did you feel me? And how do you see me now?"

She swallowed, took a deep breath, then hesitated. Whatever allowed her to see him was something she clearly wasn't certain she wanted to discuss, but Charles had too much at stake here for her to hold back. He needed to understand what was happening, so he could determine his options. Was he dying, or not? Did the fact that he was already in a ghostly form mean that he didn't have a choice? That one way or another, he was heading to that light?

"Tell me, Nanette."

Obviously she knew him well enough to know that he wouldn't be satisfied or leave her alone until she answered him, because she slowly nodded, then whispered, "I knew you were a ghost because I see ghosts, all the time. I'm a medium, Charles. And all of my cousins are, too. We help ghosts who are having a hard time finding the light to cross over."

Charles was speechless, but he wasn't doubtful. She was telling the truth; he knew it as well as he knew that he was somewhere between the living and the dead. The Vicknairs were mediums. He'd heard of mediums, of course, but he'd never dreamed that Nanette was one. But if she could see him now, did that mean she was supposed to make him go to the light? Wouldn't that beat all? He'd been fighting that damn light for days so he could find her, only for her to send him into it.

"I'm not crossing over, Nanette. Not yet." He shook his head adamantly as he spoke. He meant what he was saying, even if he wasn't sure whether he had the ultimate control over that decision. Sure, he'd fought it for three more days, but the lure of the light had been strong. Very strong. And he wasn't sure whether he could pass by it again without being drawn into its pull.

"You haven't been assigned to me, Charles," she said. "And you haven't been assigned to any of my cousins, either, or they'd have told me. They know I've been at the hospital every day, and they know how much I want you to make it, to stay on this side."

Charles was still confused as hell. "How would you know if I've been assigned to one of you? How do you even *get* assigned ghosts?"

She shrugged slightly. "It's difficult to explain, but we've got a process that has been handed down through generations of Vicknairs for over two centuries. We get our assignments here, at the plantation. That's why we've been fighting so hard to keep the place from being destroyed, Charles. If we lose our home, we don't know whether we'll be able to continue helping ghosts cross over."

Charles pinched the bridge of his nose, then pressed his fingertips outward across his brow. What had he done? Because he'd been so intent on sparring with Nanette, he'd put their beloved home—a home that was used to help lost spirits like him—at the top of the list of homes to be destroyed. How could she ever forgive him?

"So if I haven't been assigned to any of you, then I'm not dead, right?" He couldn't be dead. He had to stay alive, at least long enough to help Nanette save her house.

"No, you're not dead. But if it does become time for you to cross and you don't have any unfinished business, then you'll just go. You won't need a medium's help." Her eyes glistened again. "Charles, I want you to stay on this side."

"Like I said, I'm not crossing yet, not if I can help it. I've got something—no, I've got two things I need to do and I'm not about to go into that light until I've done both of them."

"We haven't received you as an assignment," she repeated. "You don't need to worry about those two things." She sounded concerned, as though by helping him complete the two items on his list, she'd be essentially sending him to the other side. But what Nanette didn't realize was that no matter the consequences, Charles was determined to accomplish both.

"These are things I need to do whether I cross or not, Nanette."

She looked apprehensive, but she nodded. "Okay."

"First I need to help you save your house. It's my fault that it's where it is on that demolition list, and I had planned on taking care of that when the society met earlier this week." He frowned. "Obviously, I wasn't able to do that, but now that I know the history behind the plantation, I think I know exactly what you and your family can do to ensure that your house remains standing."

She straightened in the bed, and Charles knew she was

hanging on his every word. But what he didn't know was whether she'd be willing to do what she had to do to save this place.

"You're going to have to trust me on this, Nan. But I swear, it's the truth. The only way you can save your home now is to get it on the National Register of Historic Places, and the only way you can do that is to let them know exactly why this house is so important to you and your family."

Nanette had already started shaking her head before Charles completed his explanation. The Vicknairs had kept their ghostly secret hidden from the public for the past two centuries, so they obviously hadn't planned on sharing the uniqueness of the place with the masses. But every way Charles looked at it, if they wanted to save it now, they didn't have a choice.

"We can't," she said. "We just can't. We've talked about this before, with Dax wanting to tell them what we are, what we do, so they'd help us save our home. But we've protected our secret for two centuries, Charles."

He could hear the panic in her voice and wished there was some way he could promise her that telling the public would be okay. Unfortunately, he had no idea if it would or not. Would it turn her beloved home into something akin to a circus show? He didn't think so. Louisianans by nature nurtured the supernatural; he could only imagine the parish embracing such a unique Creole heritage, a family's enduring pledge to help ghosts who'd lost their way. But even if they didn't embrace it the way he expected, that didn't matter. Because if Nanette didn't share the secrets of the plantation, she wouldn't have a home at all.

"Charles, we can't," she repeated.

"I'm sorry, *chère,* but if you want to save this place, you don't have a choice."

10

NANETTE STARED AT CHARLES in disbelief. The week had definitely taken its toll, what with the first days of school combined with his accident. And now he was proposing adding even more tumult to the whirlwind of events that had occurred in the past five days. Tell the world their secret? How could she?

"Nanette, let me explain." He moved even closer to the bed, and she fought the urge to reach for him, to touch him, the way she longed to. Touching a spirit was against the rules, and yet if she could only touch him, she believed her world would seem a little bit better. Or a lot better. She needed strength, and heaven knew, she didn't have much left. How could she divulge the family secret? What would the powers that be think if she did? Did she dare find out?

"Because of me, your plantation is on the line for demolition," he said, those charcoal eyes even more intense than usual. "I hate that, but I can't do anything about it now. I'd never planned on it getting this far, *chère,* believe me. Hell, I just wanted to spend time with you, any way I could, and since your hatred for me was palpable, I thought that arguing about your house was the only way to do it. Looking back, I realize that wasn't the wisest of ways to get close to you, particularly since you wanted to attack me any time I came around, but hell, it seemed to work for a while." One side of his mouth quirked up in the grin that had always made her weak-kneed, and his devil's dimple winked at her.

"You wanted to be close to me," Nan said, trying to put the pieces together. It had seemed as though he hadn't wanted anything more than to torment her for the past three years.

"I knew you hated me, knew you had every reason to hate me after I left you without any explanation, but I still wanted you. And I kind of hoped that eventually, my magnetic charm would lure you back in." That dimple creased deeply when he smiled, and Nanette suddenly recalled the way his face had been sliced in the accident. That dimple was most likely gone altogether. Her entire body shivered, realizing that this could very well be her last conversation, her last time ever, with Charles Roussel. Gage had been right at the hospital. There was something between her and Charles, and she had to tell him the truth about how she felt.

"After you went back to Mississippi, and when I never heard from you, I hated you."

"I know, and there's something I need to explain to you, about why I didn't come back."

She shook her head. "No. That's just it. You don't need to explain. It was a long time ago, and I wouldn't let myself get over the hurt, wouldn't even allow myself to admit that I still wanted you, regardless of whatever happened back then. I should have at least tried to talk to you, to tell you that I still cared for you. Then maybe we'd have gotten together sooner, and maybe you wouldn't be in that hospital now and—"

Nanette's heart skittered in her chest and she looked away, taking a moment to compose herself before continuing. "So, you seriously want me to tell the members of the National Register that our house is a stopping point for ghosts on their way to the other side?"

"Before I got here Tuesday night, I ended up at the meeting of the historical society, the meeting that I usually chair, and they stated that your home was definitely on the list to be destroyed, unless, by some miracle, it ended up getting on the National Register. Nanette, you know that lots of plantations apply for historical-landmark status every year, and most of their requests are refused. However, homes that are income-producing, such as a bed-and-breakfast or, given your ghostly visitors, a haunted plantation, are bumped to the very top of the list. Those are must-sees for tourists and therefore extremely beneficial to the Register. You'd be approved within days, and that's all you have, Nanette."

She felt sick. How could she betray her ancestors that way? Turning the home they'd cherished for over two hundred years into some kind of freak museum? "I—don't know if I can." It was the truth. Plus, even though she was the oldest Vicknair, she couldn't make a decision this crucial on her own. All of her cousins would need to weigh in, as well as her parents, and her aunts and uncles.

He stood and closed the distance between them, shifting from the chair to the bed. Ghost or not, heat radiated from the mesmerizing male, the way it'd always radiated from Charles, and Nanette's awareness of his presence magnified. He was here, with her, and she really didn't want to talk about the house anymore.

She wanted…Charles.

"I can't touch you," she whispered, both because she needed him to know, and because her hands were clutching the sheet in a determined effort not to reach for him. "I want to, but I can't." He hadn't been assigned to her, so Nan wasn't even sure the no-touching rule applied, but she couldn't risk him being taken away.

"I didn't tell you the second thing I need to do before I cross." His face was so close to hers that she became lost in those smoky gray eyes. They weren't black, like every other ghost she'd seen, but they were darker than usual, almost the color of storm clouds. Exhilarating. Breathtaking.

"What's the second thing?" she asked, her voice quivering due to her desperate need. Every molecule in her body prickled with anxiety, with a yearning to have this man again, in case this was their last chance. Her skin tingled, nipples ached to be kissed, and her sex became drenched in anticipation of feeling him inside of her again.

"The second thing I need, *chère,* is you. And you don't have to worry about touching me," he added, that wicked grin making her feminine center clench. "I'll touch plenty for both of us. And trust me, we'll both be very satisfied." He leaned toward her while Nanette gripped the sheet tightly, determined not to give in to the urge to break that rule. Then he gently eased his mouth across hers, the slow sensation extremely erotic, teasing her into wanting to feel that delicious touch everywhere.

A moan of longing purred in her throat. Nanette slid her eyes closed, then opened her mouth in silent invitation, wanting him to take the kiss further, to ease his tongue inside and join with her, first in their kiss, and then in much more. She needed it, ached for it, didn't think she could go on without it.

She sensed, then felt, his smile against her mouth, and whimpered when he broke the kiss. Opening her eyes, she lost herself in the dark charcoal of his. Why was he stopping?

"Last time, I took you without asking, while you thought you were asleep," he said, his voice husky, raw and aroused. "This time, I want to hear you say it, *chère*. Tell me you want this. Tell me you want me."

"I want you, Charles," she panted, barely able to say the words with her body on fire, literally aching to have what he alone could give her. She'd never wanted any other man the way she'd wanted Charles. Ever. Although she'd tried to fight it, it'd always been him. And, Nanette knew, it always would be. Even if he crossed over, even if this was their last chance, their last moment in time, she'd never want a man as much as she wanted him now. "Charles, please. I need you."

"Oh, *chère,* I've waited years to hear you say that again." He kissed her, and there wasn't anything soft about it this time. He captured her mouth deliberately, purposefully, his tongue parting her lips and sweeping inside in hungry urgency. His desire fed her own, and she squirmed beneath him, pushing the sheet away in an effort to remove all obstacles between them.

Charles eased away from her, stood beside the bed and removed his shirt. Nanette absorbed the steely contours of muscle and man, the dark flat nipples, already hard buds, the thin strip of dark hair that started just beneath his navel and disappeared beneath the waist of his pants. Nanette moistened her lips as she watched his long-fingered hands move to that waist, unbutton his pants, then slide the zipper down.

"I thought the other night, when I saw you…" She stopped, captivated as she watched him drop the pants to the floor and step out of them.

"When you saw me…" he prompted, lifting the band of his black boxer briefs to clear the head of his penis, as big and broad as it'd been the other night. Have mercy.

"I thought I was dreaming, because I didn't remember you being so—" She sucked in a breath when the boxers joined his pants on the floor "—so big."

His laugh was a low rumble that caused those ripped abs to dance wickedly in the moonlight. "You're doing incredible things to my ego, Nanette."

She smiled, knowing his ego had never suffered from lack of attention. Every woman in the parish had commented at one time or another about Charles's campaign poster. He was the prime beauty shop fodder at Monique's salon, and more than a couple of Monique's patrons had mentioned wanting to swipe a poster or two and use it for inspiration when their significant others didn't do the trick. Charles Roussel, Acadian perfection, simply had that effect on women. But he was the only man who'd ever had that effect on Nanette. And judging by the way his penis was practically straining, big and bulging and glorious, for attention, she'd say she also had that effect on him, particularly since the end of that prominent feature held a glistening drop of desire…for her.

Nanette edged toward him. "I want to taste you," she whispered, her voice deeper than normal due to her arousal.

He stepped toward the bed, but stopped just shy of her reach. "On one condition."

She could barely halt her progression. *No.* No conditions. She wanted to lick him, suck him, devour him. And then she wanted to feel every inch of him plunging deep inside of her. "Condition?"

"I want you naked first."

Smiling, Nanette edged up on her knees, fingered the lacy hem of her black nightie, then pulled it over her head. She tossed her hair, enjoying the way it felt grazing her naked back and breasts, and then looked at him, his eyes smoldering as he stared at her boldly. "Panties, too?" she asked. She'd worn the sexy nightie and thong with the hope that he'd find his way to her tonight. She'd hoped, but she hadn't truly expected it to happen. When he hadn't shown last night, she'd thought she'd lost her chance to be with him. But tonight, they were together. And if she might only be with him once more before he crossed over for eternity, then she'd make it something worth remembering. She toyed with the tiny strip of black satin at her waist. "Do you want me to take this off, too?"

The moisture at the tip of his penis increased as she taunted him, and Nanette felt oddly empowered by her ability to make it happen. "Take it off," he said, "and then, finish what you started."

She cocked a brow at him, and was rewarded when he pleaded, "Please, *chère*. I'm dying here."

Those last three words sent a painful reminder of the truth to her heart, but she fought to keep the impact of them off her face. Instead, she eased onto her back, lifted her hips and slid the scrap of satin and lace to the floor, while Charles emitted something close to a growl.

"Now?" Nanette asked, reverting to her previous position, her knees on the mattress and her face merely inches from the broad, glistening head of his penis. "Can I taste you now, Charles?"

He didn't answer, but moved toward her, while Nanette opened her mouth to take him in, then hummed her contentment when she licked the dewy head. Her hands braced her weight on the mattress, and she mentally reminded herself not to break the rule. No matter how badly she wanted to stroke his length with her grasp, fondle his heavy balls while she took him in, she couldn't. Which didn't mean that she couldn't touch him everywhere; it simply meant that she'd have to make really good use of her mouth. Worked for her. And from the way Charles's hands gripped her hair, massaging her scalp and neck and shoulders as she drew his length into her throat, it worked for him, too.

Nanette stroked him with her mouth and tongue, enjoying the way the slick heat tensed against her touch. He was fighting for control, and she was determined to make him lose the fight. She swirled her tongue around the head, then kissed the tip before blowing a stream of cool air on the dampened flesh, while he hissed in a ragged breath.

"*Chère,* if you keep that up, I'm not going to last long."

"Good. Then you can go again."

Again, that deep laugh warmed her senses, as did his hands, now tangling in her hair as he gently guided her mouth back to his cock.

"You have no idea how hard it was to get back to you," he said huskily.

Nan slid her mouth down his length then opened her lips to surround his swollen sack. She licked him languorously, purring with delight when she felt his penis move in response.

"Enough, *chère.*" His hands smoothly tilted her head so that she peered up at him.

"I wasn't finished."

His eyes were heavy lidded, his jaw tight, his control on the brink. "*Mon Dieu,* if I let you finish, I may never get to start. And I won't leave tonight without having you, *chère.*"

The finality of his statement caused her heart to thud thickly in her chest. When he left tonight…he might never get to come back. His hands slid from her hair down her neck, then his fingertips feathered across her breasts, before he shifted forward and lifted her completely, then settled her in the center of the bed.

"My turn." He indicated the headboard. "If you want to stick to that no touching rule, maybe you should hold on to something."

Nanette brought her hands above her head and fastened them around the edge of the wooden headboard. He was right. With the way her body was already burning, yearning to lose control, she might not be able to stop herself from reaching for him. She wanted to touch him desperately.

Nanette worried her lip—but then Charles settled his hard, massive body beside hers on the bed, and all worries were gone. She wouldn't think about the rules now. Right now, she'd only think about the man whose eyes were drinking her in, and whose fingers were teasing her breasts with tender caresses.

"You're beautiful, *chère.*" That thick Cajun drawl had entranced her as a teen, and still did. The voice matched the man, sinfully sexy with the promise to please. "You know, turnabout is fair play." He massaged her breast, plumping up the nipple then placing his mouth over the swollen tip while Nanette lost herself in the wet warmth of his tongue on her sensitive skin. Both of his hands were busy now, one massaging the breast he was kissing and the other massaging the one that was waiting for his mouth's attention. And Charles didn't fail to deliver. When he'd finished suckling the first, he moved to the second and gave it the same exclusive consideration. Nanette's sex throbbed for that talented mouth, and for the hard length currently pushing against her thigh.

If she could touch him, she'd take her hand to that gloriously large shaft and caress the satiny skin that she'd felt on her tongue moments ago. She'd wrap her hand around the breadth of him and stroke him, slowly at first, then faster, while knowing that she'd soon feel that sinewy length of him deep, deep inside. But because she couldn't touch, she had to grab the headboard and surrender complete control to Charles, and he was totally taking advantage of her dilemma, smiling as he kissed his way down her abdomen and she writhed wildly.

"Charles, please," she begged, the tension increasing exponentially as he slid his tongue into her navel, chuckling lightly when she gasped. Her sex dripped. "I want you inside of me."

He'd edged his way down the bed in order to move his mouth over her body, and the new position had taken that rock-hard flesh away from her completely. Nanette didn't like it, at all.

"Like I said, *chère,* turnabout is fair play. You tasted me, now I'm tasting you." He parted her curls with his fingers, and she could feel her swollen lips, damp and ready, pulse at the tender touch.

Nanette couldn't wait. She opened for him, easing her legs wide and lifting her hips to give him better access. Blessedly, he brought his mouth to her intimate flesh, the warmth of his tongue tracing a path from her clitoris to her wet opening and back again. He growled appreciatively, and that growl sent her ever so close to the edge. She hovered on the brink, a heavy wave of tension building within her, bearing down toward the very spot where his mouth touched her, kissed her, licked her. She held nothing back—she wanted to come for him, like this, with his mouth on her, bringing her where he wanted her to go, and she arched her back, pushing her hips upward and boldly pressing her clit toward that talented mouth, until he grazed it with his teeth, and Nanette plunged powerfully over the crest. Wave upon wave of pent-up pleasure found its way to the surface and tingled for release.

"Inside me, please, Charles, *please.* I want you."

Her eyes found his, and she vaguely realized that his very presence illuminated the two of them completely. He was glowing more brilliantly than before, and the pure light made the experience even more beautiful. She was making love with the man she'd wanted for as long as she could remember, and she never, ever wanted to forget. "Please," she repeated.

Charles moved above her, his muscles rippling beneath the surface, a vivid portrayal of his masculinity, his power, his virility. A trickle of moisture eased from her core, and Nanette audibly pulled in a lungful of air as he pressed his hardness between her legs. He shifted his weight, taking one hand between them to guide his length, and Nanette moaned in frustration as she realized he wasn't entering her yet.

"Charles," she panted, but she couldn't say anything more. Her mind and body were lost to what he was doing, stroking her clit with the thick head of his penis.

"Come for me again, *chère*."

He rubbed against the swollen crest, and the sensation was even more exhilarating because of how he was touching her. He could easily slide down her folds and plunge inside, but he was holding his own pleasure at bay and keeping her on the edge of orgasm.

He pressed more firmly against her as he continued to massage her clitoris with his penis. It was more than she could take, her emotions combining with the physical to bring her entire body into a tense, need-to-come-now state that had her heels pressing into the mattress, her hands gripping the headboard until her knuckles were numb, and her entire body on red alert, eager to reach what was oh so close.

"Charles, I'm going to—I'm about to—" The spiraling tension built to a fever pitch, her stomach dipped in and she hissed a ragged breath. "Charles!"

His growl joined her scream, and he grasped her hips and urged them upward, sliding his hardened length down her dampened folds, then, to Nanette's delight, pushing deep within her and sending her into wild tremors of ecstasy. She let the climax soar, yelling his name again and again as he thrust into her. She reveled in the way the inner walls of her body flexed greedily around him, determined to hold him inside of her as long as possible. He pushed, and she fought to hold on. With every withdrawal, she yearned to have him back, touching her deeper than anyone ever had, both emotionally and physically, and filling her completely the way only he could.

"Mon Dieu!" His hands gripped her hips harder, and his magnificent body shuddered as he exploded within her. Nanette's heart pounded wildly in her chest, thrilled at the incredible vision of Charles Roussel in the throes of climax, and at the sweet, intimate shudders of their orgasms fusing together to form a powerful, memorable bond.

His eyes met hers, and Nanette was pierced by their darkness, no longer gray or charcoal, but jet-black. And his body was no longer shimmering slightly, but was practically blazing with an ethereal glow.

Too late, she realized what that meant. He was getting closer to the light, closer to the other side, closer to leaving her completely.

"Charles!" she screamed, and her hands released the headboard and reached for him. "No!"

But even though she still shuddered in the aftermath of their climaxes, and still felt the heat of him on her flesh, he was gone.

_11_

STANDING ON THE PLANTATION'S porch, Nanette concentrated on lifting the heavy mug to her lips, then took another sip of the way too strong, way too hot coffee. It scalded her tongue and sizzled her throat before slamming a powerful shot of caffeine to her stomach. She winced throughout the potent liquid's journey but took another sip. She had to stay awake, somehow, in case the hospital called. And she had to be here when her cousins arrived for the ritual Saturday workday.

Today would start with a proposal that would probably shock them to shreds. Or wait—when she told them that she was in love with Charles Roussel and that she'd probably killed him with sex last night—_that_ might shock them more.

She moved beyond sips and took a huge gulp of the scorching coffee at the same moment that Gage's truck started up the driveway. Nanette had known he'd get here first. She'd left—what?—twenty messages on his pager? Maybe more. She'd stopped counting.

He climbed out of the truck and slammed the door, then stormed toward the porch. The pale blond streaks in his brown hair caught the early morning sun and for some reason reminded Nanette of how Charles had shimmered when he'd appeared in her room. But he hadn't been shimmering when he left; he'd practically been on fire, glowing so brightly that she could hardly look at him.

Her eyes burned, but she wouldn't allow the tears to fall. Which made them burn more. She gulped more coffee and glared at her cousin. "Why weren't you at the hospital last night?" Her throat stung as she spoke, probably because there wasn't much left of her esophagus after all the throat-blistering coffee.

Gage stopped short as he neared the porch, his blue eyes wide as he studied her, and at once all signs of anger disappeared. "When's the last time you slept?"

"I asked you a question."

"Contrary to popular belief, I don't live at the hospital. After working twenty-four hours straight, I went home, took the phone off the hook and spent the night with Kayla. Unfortunately, the baby kept her up most of the night again with all of his kicking, so I let her sleep this morning. She'll come over after she wakes up to help with the house." He grinned. "She's been feeling the baby move for a while now, but last night was the first time *I* actually felt him kicking. I'd press my hand on her stomach, and he'd push right back. Pretty damn cool. By the way, I got all your messages this morning when I checked my cell and my pager. I started to call you before I came over, but I was hoping you'd wised up and finally gone to sleep." He shrugged. "Should've known better."

Nanette's hand trembled around the cup. She shouldn't have jumped on Gage for spending a night at home with his pregnant wife. "I'm sorry. I didn't even think about how I might be disturbing you and Kayla on one of your rare nights off." Nanette suddenly felt swamped with guilt and *that* was what finally sent her tears over the edge. "I'm so sorry."

Before she could say another word, Gage was on the porch, taking her coffee mug and placing it on a table then wrapping her in his arms.

"Damn, cousin," he whispered against her hair. "I can't remember the last time I saw you cry, and I sure as hell have no recollection of the last time I heard you apologize."

Oddly enough, she couldn't hold back a smile at his comment. "Am I that bad?"

"No, you're that tough, or that stubborn. Take your pick."

"I need my coffee." She was having an extremely tough time pulling her eyelids back open with every blink, and she couldn't lose her battle with sleep. She had too much to do. Squirming out of his arms, she reached for the mug, but Gage shook his head and guided her to one of the porch rockers.

"You don't need coffee. You're going to tell me everything, and then you're going to bed. When's the last time you slept?"

"I slept last night." She had, some, maybe an hour or so before Charles had showed up in her bedroom.

"I know better. You were at Ochsner most of the night, because you damn near terrorized Hank."

"Hank?"

"Hank Simone, the newest doctor at the hospital. He's the one that you evidently grabbed and shook when he didn't let you in the CCU. It was a damn good thing he knew we were related, and that I'd told him how upset you were over Charles's condition."

Nanette distinctly remembered trying to barrel past a doctor when he'd blocked those blasted CCU doors. He hadn't weighed nearly as much as she'd expected. Or maybe her frustration had caused her to experience one of those adrenaline surges that helped mothers to lift cars to save their kids. Except in this case, she'd lifted a doctor and shaken him like a rag doll when he wouldn't let her pass. But Charles had been on the other side of those doors, and she…

"I wanted to be with him, hold his hand when he crossed." Her voice was watery, dismal and grim—exactly how she felt.

"Charles is still here, Nanette."

"I know. But your doctor friend—Hank—told me he's worse. And then he said that they wouldn't be allowing visitors back this morning, which just confirmed it. Charles is worse, and it's my fault." She'd needed so desperately to talk to Gage last night, but she'd only had that young doctor around, and he hadn't told her nearly enough. She had felt so *alone.*

He picked up her mug. "Listen, you sit down and relax a minute while we wait on the others to get here. I'm going to get me a cup of coffee and then I want to talk to you about blaming yourself. I know you said you were on the phone with him, but you didn't cause the accident, and you're definitely not the reason he's worse."

He turned and disappeared through the front door, while Nanette sagged in the rocker. Gage didn't understand. He thought she was still blaming herself for the accident; he didn't realize that she'd done something much worse now. Her being with Charles last night had drained him. And it was her fault for not realizing what would happen. Tuesday he'd only been with her for a short while, and yet he'd been worse on Wednesday. How bad was he today, after spending such a long time with her? Why hadn't she remembered that interacting with the living weakened spirits?

Nan winced. She knew exactly why she hadn't remembered; she hadn't wanted to. She'd only wanted to be with Charles, no matter what. And because of that, she may have given him no chance to survive.

A sob that sounded like a wounded animal pulled from her throat. Thank God Gage hadn't returned to hear it, or he'd add something else to his "I can't remember the last time I heard you do that" list.

Tires crunching on gravel brought her attention to the driveway. Tristan's Jeep was in the lead, followed by Ryan's work truck and Dax's Beemer. Nan lifted her arm to look at her watch, and even that seemed difficult in her sleep-deprived state. Eight o'clock on the nose. She smiled softly. The Vicknairs were all busy, that was for sure, but they never let each other down on their workdays. More crunching gravel signaled the arrival of the youngest cousin. Jenee had the farthest to drive from Chalmette, but she was also here every Saturday. Nan's heart warmed at the sight of all of them climbing out of their vehicles in their work clothes, ready to tackle whatever she had on the list of things to do for the day. Little did they know, today's activities weren't going to be anything like what they were expecting.

Nanette didn't want to believe it herself, but Charles had told her the truth. Unless they shared their secret, they'd lose their house. She'd spent this morning on the phone with her folks, making sure they were okay with everything she had in mind. They'd given her their approval a hundred percent, and they'd also promised to call her aunts and uncles to get their okay, as well. Within a half hour of Nan hanging up the phone, her father had called back and said that all of the older Vicknairs agreed that opening the house, and its secrets, to the public was the only way to go.

Now to tell her cousins that after two hundred years of hiding what they did, what they were, the Vicknair secret would be unveiled.

"What, no big list waiting for us at the kitchen table?" Tristan asked, climbing the porch steps with Chantelle by his side.

"Not yet," Nan said, deciding to explain when they all reached the porch.

Ryan was right behind Tristan and Chantelle with a tool belt strapped to his waist and a smile on his face.

"Monique will be here later. She's hitting a sale at the Mommy and Me store in La Place." He indicated his truck bed, where a couple of hammers were currently hovering in midair. "But I brought some additional help. They work hard, even if you won't be able to see them. That's Sam and Brian."

As Dax and Celeste passed his car, they turned toward the airborne hammers and nodded. "Glad you're here," Dax said, while Celeste smiled toward the ghosts.

Jenee chatted on her cell phone as she neared the steps. Her smile said she was talking to her fiancé, and she paused in the conversation to verify Nan's suspicion. "Nick says hi," she said, then added, "I love you, too," before disconnecting and joining the others.

The majority of the family was so absorbed in visiting with each other that they didn't truly notice Nan wasn't her usual self. However, Jenee's social-work training obviously kicked in, because she barely cleared the top porch step before gasping, "Oh, Nan! You look terrible! Did Charles cross?"

Leave it to the youngest cousin to zone in on Nanette's worst fear.

"No," Gage said, exiting the house with a steaming cup of coffee in his hand. "He hasn't gone over yet, but his condition is worse this morning, and as you can probably tell, so is Nanette's."

"Thanks," Nanette mumbled and rubbed her forehead, while Gage took a sip of his coffee, then darted to the side of the porch and spewed it.

"Hell, Nanette, that's the worst stuff I've ever had in my mouth!" His face reminded Nanette of when he was little and Grandma Adeline had suspected he'd swallowed a bit of window cleaner. She'd given him castor oil to "make sure he got rid of it," and Gage had looked…like he looked right now.

"Remember that castor oil?" she asked, and he glared at her.

"How many scoops of coffee did you use?" he asked.

"I didn't measure."

"I'd go pour it down the drain, but I'm afraid it'd eat up the pipes," he said, tossing the remainder of the thick liquid off the side of the porch. "If you need that crap to keep you awake, then you're in worse shape than I thought."

"I can't sleep, not until I talk to all of you about the house."

"What about the house?" Tristan was propped against one of the porch columns, but he straightened at the mention of their beloved plantation. "Something to do with the inspection?"

Nan nodded. "I don't really have a list of things for us to do around here today, because it doesn't really matter what we fix before next Saturday's inspection. The historical society has us on the bottom half of that list, and there's only one way for us to get moved up and save the house."

Everyone's attention turned to Nanette.

"Okay, we're listening," Dax said. "What do we have to do?"

"We have to get on the National Register of Historical Places." It sounded simple as she said it, but she knew—and they knew—that there wasn't anything simple about it.

"We've already submitted our nomination packet," Jenee said. "And the historical society knows that. We can't help that it takes time for the folks at the Register to make a decision."

"Yes," Nan said. "We can. Or rather, we can make it so blatantly obvious that we belong on that list that they can't refuse our nomination."

Nanette opened her mouth to explain how, but Dax already knew where she was headed and beat her to the punch.

"You've decided to tell them about the ghosts," he said.

"It's our only chance of saving the plantation."

"How do you know?" Chantelle asked. Even though she'd married into the Vicknair family, Chantelle understood how important keeping their secret had been to the family for the past two centuries. In fact, she probably understood better than most because she'd seen how the plantation and the family's ability to communicate with spirits had helped her sister make it to the other side.

"I know because Charles told me."

There was a slight pause in the conversation, then Gage cleared his throat. "That's what he was talking to you about when he wrecked? Is that why you're feeling so guilty about all of this, Nanette? He'd decided to help us, and then he crashed. Because even if that is what he called to tell you that day, the accident still wasn't your fault."

Nanette shook her head and tried to gather her bearings, which was difficult since she was so thoroughly exhausted. "He didn't call me that day, I called him. And that isn't when he told me. He told me last night." She didn't wait for questions before explaining. "His spirit came to me last night, and he told me that he wanted to help us save the plantation."

"Charles came to you last night," Dax repeated, then exchanged looks with his wife. Celeste frowned at her husband. Because of their own history, they knew exactly what that meant. When Celeste had been dying, her spirit had continued to find its way to Dax, and she'd nearly lost the chance at life on this side.

Exactly what Charles had done. And Nanette hadn't done a thing to stop it.

Celeste's dark green eyes turned from her husband to Nanette, and Nanette nodded, ashamed.

"I weakened him," she whispered. "I remembered what happened with the two of you, but only after he'd spent most of the night with me. I'm afraid that now—now he won't have a choice but to cross."

"Hey, Celeste stayed on this side," Dax said soothingly. "Charles doesn't *have* to cross."

"If his spirit is not strong enough to withstand the light's pull, then you know he will. And I—" she swallowed, knowing she had to tell them how much Charles meant to her, and how miserable she'd been fighting it for so long "—I love him."

12

Nanette was shocked at the family's response to her declaration of love for Charles Roussel. They stood around her and merely nodded, as if they'd known all along.

"You're not surprised," she said.

"No. The only thing that's surprising is how long it took you to admit it," Tristan said. "It's too bad that it took his accident to bring your feelings to the surface, but hey, sometimes it takes something life-threatening to bring everything in perspective." He looked at Chantelle, who'd been nearly murdered by a ghost before she'd admitted her feelings for Tristan.

"But I think I realized it too late," Nan said, to no one in particular.

"It isn't too late," Gage said. "I mean, yeah, his condition is worse this morning. I'm not going to lie to you about that. But I also know that he's got the best doctors around watching over him, and more than that, I know Charles Roussel. He's a fighter, and if he wants to stay on this side—if he wants to stay with you—I believe he'll do his damnedest to make it happen."

"But he doesn't know that it's lessening his chance for recovery every time he comes to me," Nan said, still feeling miserable.

"How many times has he come to you?" Jenee asked.

"Twice. Tuesday, and then again last night. Both nights that he took a turn for the worse."

"So next time he comes, you tell him that he needs to go back and let his body get stronger so he can stay on this side," Tristan said, taking on the authoritative tone typical of his fire-chief position.

But Nanette wasn't sure there was going to be a next time. What if Charles was already too weak to get back to her? She swallowed thickly and regretted all of the strong coffee she'd drunk earlier. Now the bitter taste combined with her emotional turmoil to make her feel sick.

Jenee crossed the porch and crouched in front of her. "Nan, let us take over today and you get some rest. You've been through too much, and I'm sure you're going to want to go back to the hospital tonight to see Charles. What did he say we need to do to get on that Register?"

Charles's words echoed in her thoughts, and she answered, "We have to show them that the plantation can be income-producing, like a bed-and-breakfast, or a—" another thick swallow "—a haunted estate."

Jenee just nodded, as did the rest of the family.

"We'd have to document our plans in an addendum to our nomination packet, and then we'd also have to show them that we're acting on those plans, that we've got things in motion to start," Nan summed up, then asked, "You're all okay with this?"

"Hey, I wanted to add those letters from the attic to our original nomination," Dax pointed out. "They prove that the Vicknairs were helping ghosts during the Civil War. We can include copies of them in the addendum."

When Nan and Dax had been searching for answers about why Celeste was stuck in the middle, they'd found several letters detailing the relationship between their great-great-great-great grandparents, Clara and John-Paul Vicknair, when John-Paul was wounded and near death in the Civil War. Dax was right; those letters would definitely add to the authenticity of their claim.

"And if we're going to let the public know, anyway, then we might as well let them really see things in action," Tristan said. "Maybe not a full-fledged bed-and-breakfast in the beginning, but we could offer tours of the place, and if a letter happened to show on the tea service when they're in Grandma Adeline's sitting room, it wouldn't really hurt anything, would it?"

"As long as none of the folks touring the place had a heart attack," Gage said, smirking. "But I agree, that'd only add to the appeal." He shrugged. "Besides, we'll have a doctor around if we need one."

"I can let my construction ghosts work on the place while the tours are in progress," Ryan said. "I don't imagine anything could lend more credence to the place being haunted than a few tools floating around." He turned and looked beyond them, toward his truck. "Sam and Brian think most construction guys would be willing to help, that it'd give them another way to show off their talents before they cross." Ryan's attention moved toward the steps and then to the front door, which opened for a moment, then closed again. "They're going on up to the attic to finish what they started the other day."

Nanette knew that tourists would eat up the opportunity to see evidence of real spirits working around the place.

How many people wondered if there truly was life beyond this world? And how many people would be willing to venture to their plantation to find out for sure?

Probably plenty.

But there was still one more problem. "We've only got a week before the next inspection. If the Historical Register doesn't approve us, and approve us fast, then we could still lose everything even if we do have a plan for converting the house into a tourist attraction."

"We need to have something like an open house by next weekend," Jenee said. "And we'll have to advertise it."

"Every dime we've got has gone into repairs," Dax said. "We're tapped out, and advertising costs money."

Tristan's head jerked toward Chantelle. "Wait a minute. Advertising does cost money, but interviews are free."

Chantelle beamed at him. "I hadn't even thought of that."

"What?" Nan asked.

"My interview. I have an interview scheduled for Monday with the *Times-Picayune.* They're running it in the Wednesday paper. The journalist wanted to talk to me about the success of my first book locally and about my upcoming projects, but I could easily mention the plantation, and the fact that the Vicknairs were the inspiration for the mediums and ghosts in my book."

"And…" Tristan prompted his wife.

She cocked her head, apparently not seeing where he was headed.

"What about the book you've been hiding?"

"Hiding?" Nan asked.

Chantelle's cheeks turned pink, and she glanced at Nanette. "I wasn't even going to show it to my editor unless you said it was okay, and I hadn't found the right opportunity to ask you how you felt about it. But I am really proud of it."

"What is it?" Nan asked, her curiosity rousing at their vagueness.

"It's a book about the Vicknair family history," Tristan said proudly. "But it's a real account, from when our ancestors came to Lafayette, to when they moved here and built the plantation, to all of the years and mediums leading to us."

"How did you get that information?" Gage asked.

"Well, in all honesty, the majority of the ghost details are from the present. Everything prior to that is mainly a family tree of Vicknairs who have lived at the plantation. I did include an account of John-Paul and Clara Vicknair's relationship based on the letters Dax found. And of course, Lillian's crossing is detailed both from the family's point of view and mine," she added, referring to her sister.

"Chantelle could talk about that manuscript when she has her interview. It'd help get the word out about us opening the plantation to tourists. And we could add the book's possible publication as yet another item in that addendum," Tristan said.

Their positive tones as they chatted about what they all could do to increase the plantation's chances of survival warmed Nanette's heart. If everything that they were planning worked out, then how could the Register refuse their nomination?

Nanette envisioned her handsome ghost. By telling her what they needed to do, Charles had potentially saved the place she loved so much.

Now if she could only save him.

13

CHARLES WAS STILL TOO WEAK for visitors Saturday night, and to Nanette's dismay, his condition didn't improve on Sunday. Her only ray of hope came from Gage, who assured her that although he wasn't better, he also wasn't worse. Thankfully, gathering information for the addendum to the National Register nomination packet kept her fairly busy throughout the day, and being busy was good. When she wasn't busy, she found herself doing something she was all too accustomed to—worrying. Worrying about losing her house, worrying about divulging the family secret and, most of all, worrying about losing Charles.

On Monday afternoon, she mailed the overnight package to the National Register of Historical Places and prayed that they'd process it soon, as in by Saturday. She was surprised at how much information they had, particularly Chantelle's account of the family's history, and she was even more surprised that it didn't bother her as much as she'd thought it would to put that packet in the mail. There was actually a sense of relief involved with setting their secrets free, though she wasn't so certain she'd still feel relief on Saturday, at their first open house.

Nanette wasn't certain how many people would come to the "Haunted Open House." They didn't have any money for formal advertising, but Monique had posted fliers in her shop, and Kayla, Jenee and Celeste had volunteered to put them up around the parish. The big push, of course, would be Chantelle's interview in Wednesday's *Times-Picayune*. As the biggest paper in New Orleans, that one would hit multiple parishes and had a readership that put the local newspapers to shame.

The interview had occurred at the plantation that morning, and the reporter had even brought a photographer along to take pictures of the house, as well as Grandma Adeline's sitting room, the tea service, and the letters from John-Paul and Clara Vicknair. Come Wednesday, all of New Orleans would definitely know their secret.

Nanette swallowed past the nauseous feeling that came with that thought. This was something they had to do; Charles had said so. She parked her car at the hospital as the sun was going down, amazed that merely a week had passed since the first day of classes, the day of Charles's accident. So much had happened in the past seven days that she could scarcely take it all in. But through it all, she'd found Charles, and finally admitted her feelings for him.

She glanced at the tall white building composing Ochsner Hospital and wondered if she'd ever see him outside of those walls again. Then she wondered if she'd ever see him within those walls again. The doctors hadn't allowed visitors yet again this morning, and unless Charles started improving, they'd follow that precedent tonight.

Charles hadn't been with Nanette since their night together on Friday, and she'd hoped the fact that he hadn't shown up in her bedroom meant that his body was healing. But she feared that it meant the opposite—that he'd become so weak that he couldn't make his way to her, and eventually, his body would lose the fight completely.

Because of Nanette.

Her throat tightened, mouth tensed and she whispered, "Grandma Adeline, if you can hear me, please, talk to them. Talk to the powers that be for him. Ryan pleaded his case with them on his own, but I'm afraid Charles is too weak. He may not even be strong enough to let them know that he wants to stay—and he does want to stay. He isn't ready to cross, and I can't live knowing that he did because of me."

She sat in the stillness of her car and waited, but no sign of acknowledgment came. She had no way of knowing whether her beloved grandmother had heard her at all, or if her words had simply been confined to the air around her. Either way, it was merely twenty minutes until the evening visitation, and she wasn't going to be late. Even if she couldn't walk through those CCU doors and see the man she loved, she'd be as near to him as she could get.

Nanette suspected she had cried more in the past week than in her entire life, and now was no different. She exited the car and walked toward the hospital while rubbing a steady stream of tears from her cheek. Thankfully, her waterworks ended by the time she stepped off the elevator and saw Johnny Roussel in the waiting room. Each night, there had been fewer and fewer members of Charles's family at the visitation hour. Nanette assumed it was due to him rarely being able to have visitors. People worked, or had children, or other things that kept them from being able to plan their lives around the off-chance that they'd get to go beyond those doors. It didn't surprise Nanette overly much that Charles's brother was the only one there tonight.

Johnny looked up when she neared, and his gray eyes, so similar to Charles's, were filled with compassion. "Looks like it's just us tonight."

"Have you seen Gage, or any of the other doctors, yet?" she asked, unable to remember whether Gage was working or if he was off. She was sure he'd probably told her, but her concentration wasn't exactly a hundred percent lately.

Johnny frowned and shook his head. "No one yet."

She nodded and sat beside him. This was the first time the two of them had been completely alone since the accident, and there was a sense of awkwardness to their solitude. Nanette recalled Johnny's words from the other night.

I know that the two of you were closer than anyone else realizes.

Nanette wondered just how much Johnny did know. She turned toward him and noticed that his eyes were focused on those closed doors. They only had a few minutes before visitation began, and she decided not to waste the opportunity to ask him. "You said you knew we were close."

His mouth quirked to the side, lower lip rolling in as though he were regretting the statement. "You know, it really isn't my place to say anything, Nanette. I mean, my brother must have a reason for never talking to you about it all, after he got back from Mississippi. But now…" He took a deep breath, shook his head. "Hell, he may never get the chance."

Nanette held her breath, uncertain that she wanted him to continue. Charles had said that he wanted to tell her something, something about what happened back then, when he was with her Friday night, but Nanette had stopped him, not wanting the past to interfere with what they were about to share. She didn't think it was right to learn whatever it was from someone else, even his brother. If she let Johnny talk to her about whatever happened, then that would essentially be saying that she didn't think Charles would ever get the opportunity to tell her himself.

And she wasn't giving up on him. Not now. Not ever.

"Don't tell me," she said resolutely. "I'll wait and get him to tell me, when he's better."

A rough sigh escaped Charles's brother, and he nodded. "I understand, and I didn't mean I was giving up on him. He's a fighter, always has been, always will be. But—well—it's tough, with him being here for so many days and now we can't even see him, see if there's any improvement, or…"

Nanette leaned toward him, wrapped an arm around him. "I'm sorry, Johnny." He probably took her words in the way that any friend would say them, that she was sorry his brother was hurt, but in her heart, they meant much, much more. She was sorry he was hurt, sorry that she'd called him during that storm, sorry that she'd kept him with her for so long Friday night—a soft sob escaped her, and Charles's brother reached for her hand.

"I won't tell you everything, then," he said, his voice thick with emotion. "But I want you to know this—he didn't want you to lose your house. He'd told me that. I think, well, hell, I know that my brother was fighting you on it just to be around you more. He has a weird way of showing his emotions sometimes, and granted, that wasn't the smartest way of showing them. But he never wanted you to lose that home."

Nanette nodded, about to tell him that she knew

Charles had never intended to destroy her home, but their attention was diverted when the doors to the CCU opened, and a young doctor—Hank Simone, she now knew—stepped out.

Johnny squeezed Nanette's hand, and then they both stood to meet Hank as he neared. Hank looked at Johnny, then at Nanette and gave them a reassuring smile.

"His condition has improved a bit today," he said, but before Nanette and Johnny could get too excited, he held up his hands and added, "but he's far from out of the woods. He's still unconscious, but he is breathing on his own now, which is a good sign. So, if you want to go back and see him, you can."

Johnny nodded. "Thank God." He took a step toward the CCU and away from Nanette. Then he stopped, as though just remembering that she was there, too. "Nanette, I'm sorry. I'm just so eager to see him."

She nodded, understanding that eagerness, since she was feeling it, too. But Johnny was family, and she wasn't. However, he'd let her go back before, and since they were the only two waiting to visit, she hoped he'd let her see Charles again tonight.

"I'd like to spend some time with him on my own, first, and then you can have the remaining time. That okay by you?"

"Yes, that's fine," she said, grateful that there were only two of them tonight, and that Johnny obviously understood how much she wanted—needed—to see Charles. She'd yet to tell him the words that she'd held in her heart for so long, and she didn't want another day to go by before she said them to him. Even if he wasn't conscious, as Gage had said, there was a chance that he heard what was going on around him. And if he did, he'd hear Nanette.

Johnny disappeared through the CCU doors, and Nanette turned toward the young doctor who was looking at her as though he didn't know what to say to her now that they were alone. But Nanette knew exactly what to say.

"I'm sorry. I shouldn't have given you such a hard time the other night. Gage said you could've called security to have me removed, or even banned, from the hospital." She smiled. "I appreciate you not doing that. I'm afraid I was just a little overemotional."

"A little?" he questioned, one dark brow raised in disbelief. But then he smiled. "Dr. Vicknair told me that his family was extremely expressive with their emotions. I just never anticipated being on the receiving end of it."

Nanette winced, recalling the way she'd grabbed his scrubs and yanked him toward her as she'd demanded he let her past the CCU doors. "I really am sorry."

"Well, looks like tonight you'll get to go back without having to bowl someone over to do it." He shrugged. "Almost seems too easy, doesn't it?"

Not knowing him all that well, she wasn't certain he was joking, until he laughed.

"It's really okay," he said. "Hospitals are places where emotions just naturally run high, and doctors are trained to deal with it. It's tough to hear that something is wrong with someone you—care about."

Nanette could've told him that he had it right the first time, but she didn't. She suspected he knew anyway, after seeing how desperately she'd wanted to get to Charles.

"I'd better get back there. You can go back when Johnny comes out."

She waited, watching the doors intently until Charles's brother emerged.

"I think his color is a little better now," Johnny said, holding the door open for Nanette to enter. "But he still looks rough," he added, apparently feeling the need to warn her.

"At least we can see him now," she said, doing her best to show optimism in both her words and tone. Evidently it worked, because Johnny smiled.

"Yeah, and I'm glad for it. Okay, well, I'm heading home to see the kids before they go to bed. I'll be back tomorrow morning." He paused. "We'll probably have quite a few here then, once I let them all know they can see him again."

"I'll be here, too—whether I get to go back or not, I'll be here."

He nodded as though knowing that'd be her response. "I'll do my best to make sure you get to see him again." Then he started for the elevator, while Nanette continued toward Charles's bed.

Like last time, the thick curtains were drawn in front of his room, and Nanette pushed them aside to see Charles, lifeless on the bed. Lifeless. Pushing that thought away, she moved to one of the two stools near the bed and sat down, then gently place her hand over his. "I'm here, Charles."

She waited, concentrating to see if he had any response to her words, whether his eyes fluttered, hand moved, breathing intensified. Anything.

Nothing changed.

Biting her lower lip, she blinked past the tears and

moved closer to the bed. "Oh, Charles, I shouldn't have kept you with me so long. I should have remembered what would happen." She sobbed, then swallowed the pitiful sound. She had to be strong for him now, in case he could hear her—and she prayed he could. "Charles, if you can hear me, listen to what I'm saying. It's important. You need to rest. If you're trying to find your way back to me, don't. That's not the way for us to be together, and that's what I want, Charles. I want you, forever. I love you. I think I always have, ever since that summer so long ago, and I hate it that I fought it for so long. But if you try to get back to me again while you're in the middle, then we might not get a chance at the real thing, at spending our lives together. So please wait, and let your body heal, and then come back to me on this side."

She waited again for something, anything, to happen. And again, he remained still, with only the sounds of his steady breathing and the beeping of the machines by his bed filling the silence.

Nanette rubbed her palm over his hand while she noted the changes in his appearance since her last visit. Johnny was right; his color was definitely better, particularly on his face, where the bruises on the right side were only a couple of shades darker than his usual tan skin and his right eye was no longer swollen. The majority of the left side of his face, where that long slice had been, was still bandaged. The tube at his mouth had been removed, and thankfully, his lips had some color again.

She instantly recalled that mouth on hers, and on every other part of her, merely three nights ago. "Come back to me, Charles," she whispered, as the curtain slid loudly across the metal rod, and Hank Simone stepped into the room.

Nanette immediately looked at the clock on the wall. "There's fifteen more minutes," she said, not wanting to leave a second sooner than she had to.

"I know, but he has another visitor," Hank said apologetically. Then a petite blonde edged her way through the curtain and moved her hand to her mouth when she saw Charles.

"Charles, oh, no, Charles," she whimpered, hurriedly moving toward the bed and, ignoring Nanette's presence, leaning over Charles to place a kiss on his forehead that left a pale pink glossy imprint of her lips there.

Nanette looked at the woman, but her attention was transfixed on Charles, so Nan turned toward Hank. He frowned slightly, then left the curtained area, leaving the two women with the unconscious man.

"My brother heard about your accident and called me, and I came as soon as I heard. I wish I'd have known sooner. Oh, Charles, your beautiful face," she said, reaching out to softly touch the bandage. She looked up at Nanette. "Will he—do they know if he'll have a scar?"

Nanette blinked. A scar? Charles's life was in jeopardy, and she was worried about a scar? "No one has talked about a scar. We're just wanting him to pull through."

The blonde shook her head. "Oh, I'm so sorry. That came out totally wrong. I never could say the right thing, could I, Charles?" she said toward the bed. "He was always making fun of me when I'd mess up. In an affectionate way, I mean." She sniffed again. "This—it's just so hard to believe. Charles was always a careful driver. And he always seemed, well, you know, like he was kind of invincible. I didn't think anything could ever hurt him."

"Are you related to Charles?" Nan asked. Only family members were allowed back in CCU, or those approved by the family, like Nanette. There was no one there to approve her so this woman had to be family, but Nan was certain she'd never seen her.

"I'm Maria Roussel."

She didn't clarify how she was related to Charles, and said the name as though Nanette should recognize it, but she didn't. Charles didn't have any sisters, and Nanette didn't know of any family members named Maria. And this woman definitely didn't look like a Roussel. With their traditional jet-black hair, smoky eyes and tan skin, they all looked like true Cajuns; this woman looked like a Barbie. She was blond and tiny, with big blue eyes and porcelain skin. Her features were delicate, and they were currently covered with tears dripping freely down her pretty face.

"I'm Nanette Vicknair," Nan said, squelching the urge to add that she loved the man in the bed.

Maria daintily dabbed her tears away, then her eyes widened. "You're Nanette Vicknair?"

Nanette looked at Charles, then at the clock. She was down to ten minutes, and she really didn't want to use her time with him chitchatting with this lady, particularly when the woman seemed to come from nowhere. But she did want to know who she was, why she'd suddenly appeared, and how she knew Nan. "Yes, I am." Nan noticed the woman's gaze had moved to Nanette's hand, tenderly rubbing Charles's arm.

"He mentioned you," Maria said. "A few times, during our

first year together. That was quite a while ago, during our senior year at Mississippi State. That was the best year of my life." She glanced back at Charles, then added, "I didn't realize that you were still around." Her words were softly spoken, but Nanette detected a subtle change in the delivery.

A sick feeling inched through Nanette, and she glanced at Charles. He'd wanted to tell her something. Johnny had also tried to tell her something. She looked up at the pretty blonde, and suddenly had a feeling that she was looking at that *something*. "Your first year together?"

"The year we were married."

14

THE LIGHT WAS GETTING STRONGER, almost magnetic in its pull. Charles continued to trudge his way through the haze in an effort to find Nanette, but the cloud was so thick and cold, and the light behind him was bright and warm. But going to that warmth meant leaving Nanette for good, and he was determined to fight as long as he could. The thought of not being with her again was too painful to just give up.

Like before, time was lost in this place, and Charles would swear he'd been searching for her for years. Did spirits actually do that, hover in this middle realm in search of those they'd left behind instead of going to the light? Obviously, they did, because he sure was. He thought of all those years growing up when he'd been skeptical when his father had sworn he believed in ghosts; if Charles could talk to his dad now, he'd tell him: ghosts were real, and occasionally, they got frustrated. Like now.

"*Mon Dieu,* I just want to see her again. I need to help her family, and I need her—period. Just once more before I go. Please."

The haze thinned, and he saw the familiar door to the council chambers ahead. Okay, it wasn't Nanette's door, but the last time he'd entered the historical society's meeting, he'd learned what her family needed to do to save the house.

Apparently, there was something else he needed to find out for Nanette, then hopefully the powers that be would let him go to her. That'd only make sense—he'd learn what she needed to know, and then he'd be sent to tell her.

Charles quickly moved toward the door, eager to find out what was happening on the other side, and move on to Nanette. Like before, no sooner did he have the thought than he found himself inside the chambers. But this wasn't a typical meeting of the society, only two men were in the room. Paul Remondet and Eddie Solomon sat behind several stacks of papers, the requests for society funding, Charles realized. But they weren't looking at the request packets; they were looking at another set of documents entirely, and Eddie's weathered face broke into a grin as he read the text on one of the pages.

"Got to hand it to them. They're pulling out all the stops," he said.

Paul finished the page he was on, took the next one from Eddie and scanned it, his eyes growing bigger with every line.

"So, do you believe it?" Eddie asked.

"That the Vicknairs have sent all of this to the Register folks, or that they've really got ghosts in their attic?" Paul asked.

"Not their attic. It's their sitting room, according to this," Eddie said, still smiling in admiration.

"I reckon half of Louisiana probably has ghosts in their attic. I just don't know of anyone who can prove it," Paul replied. "But I know one thing. They sure don't want to lose that house. You know, I can see Gage Vicknair doing something like this. He always had a wild hair back in high school. But this came from Nanette, and I never figured her to do something this off-the-wall, being a high-school teacher and all. I mean, they're turning the place into some kind of a haunted house festival."

"Well, I'd pay to see if it's true," Eddie said. "I'm betting a few more folks in the parish would, too."

Charles grinned. His recommendation to Nanette just might work. He couldn't wait to tell her…and then celebrate their victory in the buff.

"She sent this over today, along with a note saying that the same thing had been mailed to the National Register Review Committee." Paul held up the large envelope that had apparently contained the copy of her addendum. "I just wanted to get your take on it before we meet with the rest of the society members tomorrow night. President Roussel had been pretty adamant in his belief that the Vicknair place should go, and I have to agree that the house couldn't survive another hurricane."

Eddie nodded solemnly. "It won't matter if they've got a real haunted house if the place falls to the ground come the first big wind, which means that we'd either have to approve them quick and get their house up to par to withstand hurricane-force winds, or we need to turn them down and tell them to leave their ghosts in the closet, so to speak."

"Which is what Charles Roussel wanted," Paul reminded him, and Charles shook his head in disbelief. They were going to tear the place down anyway, even though Nanette and her family were putting all of their secrets out there for the world to see.

"Yeah, but President Roussel didn't know the place was

supposedly haunted, or that they'd be willing to exploit that trait to put their house on the map."

"Still, it's only worthy of being on the map if it's standing," Paul said, frowning as he held up a flier for the "Haunted Open House" at the Vicknair plantation. "These are all over town, you know."

"Yeah, I saw one of them today at the gas station," Eddie acknowledged. "Saw a couple of people stop and read it."

"Even if they can fool people into thinking it might be haunted and get them to pay for a visit to the place, I don't see how we can fund the remainder of their restoration—and turn down other homes that aren't in nearly as bad a shape—unless they get approved by the National Register. Fixing up their home will take money away from other houses, and we could probably repair three of the lesser damaged homes for what it'd take to bring the Vicknair place where it needs to be." Paul looked up at Eddie. "That's what I'm planning to tell the committee at tomorrow night's meeting, that this doesn't really change anything. I just want to know if you agree that we should maintain our goal of doing what President Roussel wanted."

"No, you shouldn't," Charles practically howled, but neither heard.

Eddie nodded. "I agree, since that's what Charles recommended. But you have to hand it to them, no other family has gone to this kind of length—saying their plantation is haunted, of all things—to keep their house standing."

Paul gathered the papers and stacked them all in one place. "Unfortunately for the Vicknairs, we don't pick which houses to save based on ghost stories."

Charles watched the two men gather their things and

exit the room, and then he paused before trying to go see Nanette. He had to figure out a way to tell her that things might not go as smoothly as he'd anticipated.

No. That wasn't true. He'd known that the committee probably wouldn't bump them to the top of the list voluntarily, because, as he'd just seen in Paul and Eddie's conversation, they did respect Charles's opinion. And damn it, he'd told them that the Vicknair place needed to go. Regrettably, he had no way of telling them that he'd planned to reverse that stance at last Tuesday's meeting.

Charles concentrated, picturing Nan's bedroom. He left the council chambers—and found himself back in that endless fog. But he simply closed his eyes to try again.

He wasn't stopping until he found her.

NANETTE BARELY REMEMBERED leaving the hospital, and the drive home was a blur, with Maria Roussel's words echoing in her head.

"The year we were married."

Maria had proceeded to tell Nanette about how much she'd loved Charles, from the very first moment she'd seen him on campus. Nanette had sat stoically listening to Maria's reminiscence, and while the minutes for visitation ticked away, the pieces had all fallen, or rather, they'd dropped forcefully, into place. That summer so long ago, when Nanette had given Charles her virginity and her heart, Charles had been married. Married. To Maria.

The visitation period had ended with Maria kissing her husband again and Nanette feeling…broken. She'd been so stunned at Maria's proclamation that she hadn't thought to ask the obvious questions about her late appearance at her husband's side. Why had Maria received the news from her brother, instead of from Charles's family? Why hadn't she been living with Charles over the past few years? Why hadn't Nanette—or anyone else in the parish—ever heard of his wife? She wasn't living in the parish, or Nanette would've known. The place wasn't that big.

Nanette took a scalding hot shower and willed her muscles, her brain and her heart to relax. She had to think. Had to wrap her mind around the bizarre turn of events and figure out the truth, because she had no doubt that Maria *Roussel* hadn't told her everything. But Nanette was still too shaken. In fact, she couldn't imagine anything that would have shocked her more than learning Charles had been married back then...

Except for finding Charles waiting, naked, a sheet barely draped over his waist, in her bed.

"I made it," he said, and even in her state of astonishment over Maria's news, his appearance made her heart dance.

Then several things hit Nanette at once. First, Charles was naked in bed. Second, Charles was married, so it didn't matter that he was naked in her bed; she would never sleep with a married man. Third, hell, she'd already slept with a married man! And fourth, if she didn't send Charles back and pronto, he'd be weakened again.

Oddly enough, the one item on that list that mattered the most at the moment was keeping him strong. Even if Charles had done Nanette—and Maria—wrong, she didn't want him to cross over. She cared about him too much to let him go, even if she couldn't have him for herself.

And didn't that hurt.

"Charles, you have to leave."

His sexy smile instantly flattened, and those dark gray eyes surveyed her as though she'd lost her mind. "*Chère,* do you have any idea how hard it was for me to find my way back? This isn't exactly the welcome I was expecting, though you in a towel definitely works into my plan."

Nan tucked the towel in tighter at her chest. No way did she need to be this close to naked with a man who let his spirit roam all over heaven and creation instead of making it stay with his body—and his wife—in that hospital room.

She took a deep breath, not knowing exactly where to start. Charles, on the other hand, didn't have any problem knowing where he wanted to start. He lifted the sheet and silently beckoned her to join him.

"We can't, Charles. I can't."

"*Chère,* we already have, and I haven't stopped thinking about it since. I meant it when I said it was damn difficult to get here, and I can't believe you don't want to share another night together before I go." Then his gaze intensified, and he added huskily, "I want to love you once more, Nanette. Please."

"Charles, every time you're with me, your spirit is weakened. You might not have to cross now, but if you keep coming back to me, you're lessening your chances to stay on this side." She shook her head. "I should have remembered that before, but I was too caught up in everything to think straight. I won't make that mistake again. I can't let you lose your life because of me."

He frowned, dropping the sheet back on the bed. "Every time we're together, I get weaker?"

She nodded. "You might not have a choice but to cross if we're together again."

"But there are no guarantees. Even if we stay apart now, I may still die. That's what you're saying, right?"

"Yes, but you will lose your chance to stay altogether if you weaken your spirit to the point where you can't resist the light." She paused, praying that he understood how important this was, and also willing her body to stay put on this side of the room, in spite of how desperately she wanted to climb under those sheets and give in to the temptation to have what he offered.

He waited a heartbeat, then said, "I won't risk it, Nanette."

"Then you'll go back?" she asked, both relieved and dismayed. The thought that this could be their last time together, and that she was sending him away, made her miserable.

"No. I won't risk never having another chance to be with you, Nan. I'm here now, and I want you. Tell me you won't make me leave, not without letting me hold you, letting me have you."

Her mind yelled no, but when her body—and her heart—screamed yes, she decided that there simply wasn't any way around saying what she knew would send him on his way. She hoped this wouldn't be their last conversation, because she didn't want her last moments with Charles to be spent talking about another woman.

"I met Maria."

His jaw tightened, and his entire body tensed. "Hell."

"I can't—I won't—sleep with a married man, Charles. I wouldn't have before…if I'd known. So please. Just go."

She didn't want him to leave, didn't want this to be her last conversation with him, but in order to save him from crossing over, she needed his spirit to stay put with his body at the hospital. Once he was safely on this side for good, they could discuss what had made him keep something so important from Nanette. Right now, however, she just wanted to keep him in the land of the living, even if it meant sending him on his way.

"There's no way I'm leaving now," he said, shaking his head. "We've got a lot to talk about, and then, after we talk, we've got some additional unfinished business. I want you, Nanette, and I damn well know you want me. And I'm not leaving here until we finally work out the past, and move on to the present."

She didn't miss the fact that he didn't mention the future. But she wanted him to have one, with or without her. "We'll talk after you recover."

"Nanette, I'm not married and have never been married at any time when we've been together." He lifted the sheet and showed her pure male perfection. "Now come get in the bed, we'll talk first, and then we'll do what we both want to do."

"We can't, Charles. I was telling you the truth. It'll weaken you, and I'm not willing to do that."

He obviously disliked her response. "Then we'll just talk, but after what I went through to get here, I'm not leaving this room in any way, shape or form until I at least hold you. So let me hold you, or suffer through watching me remain in this bed until I cross."

"You wouldn't."

"I would, and you know it. I'm dying here, Nan, perhaps literally, and my last wish is to have you in my arms again, where you belong."

She couldn't have stopped her response to that. She'd

wanted to be in his arms for the majority of her life. Within seconds, she stood beside the bed. "Charles, we can't do anything beyond talking."

"I don't like it, but fine, as long as we talk naked."

She couldn't help but laugh. "You're horrible."

"Maybe, but at least I'm not married."

That got her attention. She was rather surprised with herself. She'd always thought herself something of a literalist, requiring proof of everything she was told, even when it involved ghosts and the other side. But Charles merely stated that he hadn't been married when they were together, and she believed him without another word. Case closed. That spoke volumes of her faith in him, of her trust in him. If he said something was so, then it was.

"Are you dropping that towel and climbing in, or not?" he asked, that wicked dimple winking at her with his smile. "Like I said, we have plenty to talk about, but only if you're naked, and only if you're right here." He patted the bed beside him.

Nanette dropped the towel, then stood nude by the bed while Charles's eyes scanned her from head to toe.

"If I had to die right now, I'd die happy. Not as happy as I could be, but fairly close."

Again, she laughed, and climbed in the bed beside him, careful to keep her hands at her sides and fisted. "I can't touch you."

"I remember," he said, reaching one hand toward her breast and stroking her nipple. "But I can."

She sucked in a breath when his fingers began a thorough tormenting of one breast, then the other, and her sex grew damp with building anticipation. "I thought we were going to talk."

"*Chère,* have faith in me. I can do two things at once." Then he smiled, and while he moved his massaging techniques to her side, he told her what Maria hadn't. "I'd noticed you always, as we were growing up. When I was at my grandma Roussel's place, now Johnny's place, I'd see you outside the Vicknair plantation. You had an enormous amount of energy, always running and laughing. Even when you were little, that laugh made me stop and listen. Then you grew older, and it wasn't merely your laugh that held my attention. You were compelling in a way I could scarcely comprehend as a teen, but now I understand it well. Long, silky jet-black hair that makes your fingers yearn to touch it," he said, moving a hand to her hair and gliding his fingers through its length. "A mouth that, undeniably, was made for kissing."

He ran his finger across her lower lip, then slipped it inside, and Nanette gently sucked on the tip, closing her eyes as she recalled how it felt to suck on the tip of his broad penis. Her hips naturally moved forward to nudge that hard length, and a low, guttural growl rumbled from his chest.

"You're playing with fire down there, *chère,* if you only want to talk."

"I want to finish this conversation," she said, in spite of the fact that her hips were steadily massaging his penis now, and the process was slowly but surely working her feminine center closer to where it wanted to be.

He swallowed and nodded. "Right. I have more to tell you, about back then, and about Maria. But there's nothing that says I can't touch you here while I do." His hand found its way down her abdomen and then slid between her legs.

Nanette moved one leg on top of his to give him better access, then relished the feel of his thumb stroking her clit. "Tell me—the rest," she said, barely able to speak.

"I wanted you, before I left for Mississippi. But you were too young, fourteen, and we were friends, remember? Flirting friends, but friends just the same. I wasn't about to jeopardize what we shared because I was a horny eighteen-year-old, and you were a fourteen-year-old who couldn't help it that she looked like a nineteen-year-old, and a nineteen-year-old worthy of *Playboy* at that."

Nanette smiled, both because she was pleased that he had actually wanted her back then, when she'd been so smitten with the oldest Roussel brother, and because he was stroking her toward a much needed orgasm. "You knew I wanted you," she whispered.

"You never were that good at hiding your emotions," he said. "But you were just a kid."

"But then you went to Mississippi, and I didn't even see you again until that summer, when I was eighteen."

"I didn't come home any more than necessary during my undergraduate years, not because I had anything against coming home, but because I was enjoying life. Mississippi State was everything I'd dreamed of and then some. I joined a fraternity, met a bunch of new friends and dated girls at the university."

"In other words, you forgot me."

"No, I never forgot you, Nanette. Trust me, no man who has ever met you has forgotten you. But I met other people, and I dated them. During my senior year, I met Maria."

His thumb slowed its massaging of Nanette's clit as he said Maria's name, but Nanette wasn't about to have any part of him slacking off on what he was doing. She shifted her hips to press the burning nub against his thumb, ordered him, "Don't you dare stop, I don't care what you're talking about," and was welcomed by his rumbling laugh.

"*Chère,* it should've always been you," he said, and he blessedly picked up the tempo, while his fingers slid down her folds and pressed into her slick opening.

"Why wasn't it?" she panted. "I mean, I knew you were dating. I was, too. But I always had you in the back of my mind, looking for you to show at your grandmother's place on holidays and during the summers."

"I went to school in the summer. Eager to get out and make my mark in politics, you know. Until that one summer between undergraduate and graduate school."

"When we got together."

He nodded, and Nanette felt the tension building. She was getting close.

"Maria said you were married then," she whimpered, squirming.

"I was with Maria twice, right before I left school for the summer break. But we weren't married. We barely knew each other. And then I returned home, and saw you, and wanted you more than ever. Unlike Maria, I knew you, which made our first time together that much more meaningful, even more so because it was your first time ever."

Nanette's memory of that summer, of the fairgrounds and the reflections of Charles inside her in the house of mirrors combined with the present, with him touching her, talking to her, loving her…and she couldn't hold back on her climax any longer. She sucked in a deep breath, pressed against his amazing fingers, and let her orgasm soar.

"That's it, *chère*. Let me see you come," he whispered, "the way you did that very first time, when you gave me your body, and took my heart."

Nanette's core convulsed around his fingers, a warm flood of desire bursting forth and causing her to tremble uncontrollably. Charles kissed her as she came, containing her whimpers of completion with his mouth.

"Why didn't you come back?" she asked, as soon as she could string words together in the aftermath of her climax.

He sighed thickly. "I told you Maria and I were together twice. On one of those times, she became pregnant. Or that's what she told me when I got back to school. We both knew we didn't love each other, but I couldn't stand the thought of not being there with my child. I wanted you, believed that we could have something that would last a lifetime, and had every intention of coming back to you until Maria's news."

Nanette blinked. "You have a child?"

"No. I married Maria to be with a child that never existed. She wasn't pregnant. She said she was because, well, she was obsessed with me. She knew I'd gone home and been with you over the summer. She didn't know you, but she hated you. Maria has never been all that stable, but I didn't realize that until after we married, when she said she miscarried."

"Said she miscarried?" Nanette feared she now knew exactly what had happened back then. Charles had been manipulated into marrying someone he didn't love.

"I didn't know she lied about the pregnancy, not at first. And she'd appeared so fragile after the miscarriage that I couldn't do anything but try to help see her through it, be the supportive husband, and hope that eventually our marriage would lead to love."

"It didn't."

"No. Maria wanted to be married to me, but we never loved each other. I tried my damnedest to make it work. For four years, we stayed together, until finally, during a heated argument, she blurted out the truth."

"That she'd never been pregnant," Nanette said, her heart aching for him. For four years he'd tried to salvage a marriage that was based on a lie.

"I swore that I'd never lose my head to a woman again, any woman…"

"Including me," Nanette whispered, leaning toward him to kiss him softly, and finding it nearly impossible not to unclench her fists and touch him, hold him, let him know that not every woman out there was like Maria. "You didn't trust women."

"No, I didn't. And you didn't trust men, because I never came back." His mouth crooked up on one side and he added, "Hell, I was too much of a coward to even tell you I got Maria pregnant in a letter. We wasted a lot of time we could've been together, *chère*."

"Why did she tell me she was your wife, instead of ex-wife? She acted as though the two of you were still together."

"Like I said, Maria isn't stable. And she has to be the most jealous person I've ever met, particularly toward you. I made the mistake of confiding in a friend that first year about how much I wanted you, how I'd married one girl but couldn't deny the feelings I had for another. He betrayed my confidence and told Maria, and all hell broke loose." Charles shook his head. "That's when she said she miscarried, and I think she did it then just to make me feel worse."

"Oh, Charles, I'm so sorry."

"When I got back to Louisiana to try my hand at local politics, and then I ended up in charge of the committee overseeing the potential restoration of your home, I thought I could treat you like I did every other woman. I hadn't thought any female would ever tempt me into wanting a relationship again. But I wanted you more than ever, and you hated me more than ever. I figured, hell, if I can't have you the way I want, then I'll take what I can get. And I won't deny it, *chère,* fighting with you, seeing that feisty temper of yours in action, was rather fun."

She wanted to punch him for that, but she couldn't touch him. Not with her hands, anyway. So she bit his shoulder. Hard. The head of his penis immediately stirred against her core.

"*Chère.* Don't say no."

"Charles, I want you, but being with me, just talking with me, weakens you. Making love weakens you even more. And as bad as I want it now, I'd never forgive myself if I cost us a lifetime together because I couldn't wait."

His gray eyes darkened, and she wondered how much they'd already weakened him with this visit. "A lifetime together," he repeated. "Promise me, *chère,* if I leave you now, let my body get stronger, promise me that you'll give me that. A lifetime—with you."

"I will," she said, but the man in her bed, the man in her heart, had already disappeared.

Nanette climbed naked from the bed and scrambled

across the room to grab the phone, then she hurriedly dialed the hospital and asked for Gage.

"Dr. Vicknair," he answered.

Nanette blurted out, "Charles. How is he?"

"Nanette? What's wrong? I just checked on him a little while ago, and his condition was the same."

"Check on him now, Gage. Please. Check on him now."

"Damn it. He came to you again, didn't he?"

"Just check on him, Gage. Tell me he's okay. Dear God, let him be okay."

"Hold on."

Gage was gone a couple of minutes at the most, but to Nanette, it was an eternity.

An eternity. The thought of Charles starting his eternity without her...no. She wouldn't think about that, not yet.

"Promise me that you'll give me that. A lifetime—with you."

"Say he's okay. Say he's okay," she whispered.

"Nanette."

"Gage, how is he?" she demanded frantically. "Is he—"

"Still here. His heart rate increased and was rather erratic over the past hour, according to the nurse watching his monitor, but he's okay." He lowered his voice to a whisper and continued, "Not any better, but that's to be expected, especially if he isn't allowing his spirit to rest. Did you tell him he needs to stay put? I mean it, Nanette. If the two of you can't control yourselves, at least until he's out of here, then you're risking his life. I know you understand me on this."

"I do, and we didn't do *everything,* but he was here for a while. And it's very hard to tell him no."

Gage seemed to pause at that. Finally he said, "I never thought I'd see the day when you couldn't tell anyone no, much less Charles Roussel."

Nanette could tell from his tone that he was smiling. "Just take care of him," she said. "And I promise not to excite him again."

"Good. It'll make my job a lot easier."

"You think he'll recover, don't you, Gage?"

She heard his exhalation over the line. Gage wouldn't lie to her. She knew he wouldn't. And she desperately needed to hear someone say that Charles would be okay. "Gage?"

"You know, I don't make a habit of guessing whether someone will get better. It's not smart, from a physician's standpoint."

"I know, but this time, for me, tell me what you think. Please."

"Okay. I think, as long as my patient stops allowing his spirit to leave his body and sleep with my cousin, he may find himself fully recovered soon."

She smirked toward the phone. "I said we didn't do *everything*—this time."

"In any case, yeah, I think he'll get better, if for no other reason than he'd just spent the last hour or so letting his spirit do—whatever the two of you were doing—and he's still here. Obviously, the guy isn't ready to head toward the light quite yet."

Relief washed over her, and the emotion was so potent that tears trickled down her cheeks. She sniffed, and Gage heard.

"*Mon Dieu,* you're crying again, Nanette?"

"Maybe."

"That does it. I have to get this guy well soon, otherwise I may not even recognize you as my loves-to-bitch cousin by the end of this."

"Gage?" she said sweetly.

"Yeah?"

"Bite me."

Smiling, she hung up the phone.

15

NANETTE STEPPED OFF the hospital elevator Tuesday morning and nearly ran right into Johnny Roussel, who looked as though he'd seen a ghost. She'd already checked on Charles's status this morning via Gage and knew that his condition hadn't worsened. But something had his brother worked up. "Nanette, I was watching for you," he said, while Nanette quickly surveyed the crowd of Roussels waiting by the CCU entrance. Johnny had undoubtedly told them that the doctors were allowing him to have visitors again, and they were all clearly anxious to see him. It warmed her heart to see how many people cared about him, like she did.

"Nanette," he repeated. "I need to talk to you for a moment before the visiting hour begins." He shot a troubled glance toward the CCU doors, and Nanette followed his line of sight to see Maria chatting with Hank Simone, who looked quite entranced with the pretty Barbie.

"It's okay, Johnny," Nan said, not wanting him to worry about some sort of confrontation between her and Charles's ex. "I know about Maria and Charles."

Johnny's mouth dropped open, then snapped shut, as though he wasn't sure what to say to that. Nanette thought it was adorable, the way he was obviously trying to protect his older brother, probably in the same manner that Charles had protected him throughout their youth. The two were closer than most brothers, Nan knew that from watching them grow up together, and from seeing how often Charles visited Johnny's family. Then again, now she knew that many of those visits had been for the off-chance of seeing her. She smiled, and Johnny shook his head.

"Nan, I don't think you do know. There's no way."

"That they were married, and that she lied to him about her pregnancy, primarily to keep him from coming back to me?"

Another mouth drop.

"I do know, Johnny, and I understand now why Charles stayed away, and why he didn't make any effort to set things straight when he returned. He didn't want another relationship after what he went through, and I don't blame him for that."

"How do you know all of that? And when did you find out?"

Nanette considered what she was about to say, then figured if the entire world was about to know their secret, she might as well start with her next-door neighbor. He'd see the open house going on Saturday anyway; might as well prepare him for the show. "I learned about it last night, from Charles."

"Charles didn't speak last night," he said adamantly. "He was unconscious when I left, and the doctors told me this morning that nothing had changed."

Nanette opened her purse and withdrew one of the bright yellow fliers that her cousins were posting all over the parish. "Have you seen this yet? Or heard about it?"

He took the piece of paper and read it, then nodded. "Cindy. She mentioned something this morning while we were getting ready to come here, said that she'd heard a rumor that your place was haunted and that you were going to let people come see your ghosts, or something like that." He shrugged. "I figured it was just another crazy rumor that'd been started at the high school, you know, to mess with one of the teachers."

Nan smiled. It did sound like something her students would do to get a rise out of her, but that wasn't the case. Not this time. "It's true," she said. "We're opening the house on Saturday for our first tours."

"Tours," he repeated.

"Johnny, as odd as this may sound, our house is haunted, in a sense. The Vicknairs are mediums. We help lost ghosts find their way to the light." She could see the white all the way around both of his gray eyes, and then he shook his head.

"Tell me the truth, Nanette."

"I am."

He shot another glance toward the CCU doors, saw that they were still closed, then turned back to her and seemed to process what she'd said, everything she'd said. "You said you learned about Maria from Charles."

"I did."

"You're telling me that Charles came to see you last night."

"His spirit came to see me, his body was still here."

Johnny turned so his back faced the wall, then he leaned against it, as though his solid frame would collapse if he tried to hold it up on his own. "I'd say it wasn't possible, but hell, this is the bayou, isn't it? And I've heard of crazier things than having a haunted house next door." Then he pinched the bridge of his nose. "You wouldn't know about all of that, about Maria, if he hadn't told you. He never told anyone here, because he feared the voters wouldn't understand, and he really does want to make his mark in politics. And given your past relationship, he'd *never* have told you."

"I know. But he told me last night, Johnny. I swear."

He held up a hand. "Just—give me a second here." Then he closed his eyes and nodded as though coming to grips with the information. Finally, he looked at her again. "Does that mean he's dying? Hell, Nanette, tell me that isn't why you saw his spirit last night."

She understood his fear; she felt it, too. "It just means that he has allowed his spirit to wander in the middle, and that it's up to him to keep his spirit with his body, to stay away from the light and let his body and spirit join again, to get healthy, and stay on this side."

His throat pulsed as he swallowed. "Okay. Okay, I can handle that. Charles came to see you, and he told you about Maria."

"He told me everything, and I did the same."

"You did the same," he said, sounding rather dumbstruck by the content of this conversation.

"I care about him, Johnny."

The doors to CCU opened, and Gage stepped out, said a few words to the crowd and then took the first two visitors, Charles's parents, back to see their son.

"Look at her. She blessed me out this morning because I didn't call and tell her about Charles, now she can't get her sights off that doctor long enough to realize that the visitation has started." Johnny shook his head as he glared at Maria. "She nearly ruined him, you know. He was a very bitter man when he came back here, mad at the world, and at women in general." He looked back at Nanette. "Then Katrina hit, and as bad as that was, the opportunity to fight with you on a regular basis really lifted his spirits."

Nanette had to smother her laugh. Laughing didn't seem quite right on the CCU floor, even if Johnny's statement was hilarious. "Well, I'm glad that I helped."

"You love him, don't you?"

"I do."

He nodded. "I kind of figured if Charles ever fell for anyone, it wouldn't be your typical woman. He always liked things that were, I don't know, unique. Can't get much more unique than a family that talks to ghosts."

She smiled again, truly enjoying this conversation with Charles's brother. "So, you're okay with all of this?"

"Sure, what's another ghost or two in Louisiana?" he said. "So I'm assuming he told you he wasn't going to let your place be destroyed. He'd planned to tell the society to let it stand."

"I know."

"Well, then I should tell you that I called Paul Remondet yesterday and told him that Charles had changed his mind about your place."

Nanette's attention spiked. "And?"

"And he said that if Charles had changed his mind, he'd have made sure the committee knew about it. He also reminded me that my brother always had a plan, and that they were following it." Johnny grinned. "It seemed as though he didn't think Charles *could* make a bad decision. Hell, I thought it was only the females in the parish who were so smitten with my brother."

Nan smiled. Johnny and Charles were both stunning men, but Charles had that *something,* an almost magnetic charm that lured people in, particularly females. And that allure, along with his amazing looks, had gotten him far in life, and would get him far in politics. Nanette totally foresaw that appeal taking him all the way to the White House, if that was where he chose to go. "Well, I appreciate you trying to tell Paul what Charles wanted, even if he didn't believe it."

"It'd have been better if it'd worked, but you're welcome." He glanced back at the CCU doors. "Mary stayed home with the kids this morning, so I'm on my own. With so many people here to see him, we won't get individual visits, but if you'd like, you can come back with me."

"I would like that a lot." She'd been a bit concerned that with all of Charles's family here, she might not get to see him at all.

"And on Saturday, when you have that open house thing, why don't y'all use my place for parking cars? We've got plenty of land, and I wouldn't want all of the traffic scaring your ghosts away."

Nanette wasn't sure whether he was joking or not, so she simply accepted his offer. "Thanks. That'd be great."

By the time they took their turn at going back to see Charles, Nanette could tell Johnny was totally at ease with her medium status. In fact, as soon as they moved within the curtain wall, he whispered, "Well, is he all there?"

Nanette again had to smother a laugh. "I wish I could look at him and tell, but I can't. However, he told me last night that he would try to remain on this side, and he knows that means putting a halt to his wandering spirit."

Johnny looked affectionately as his big brother. "Wandering spirit. That's what our grandmother said he had when he went to Mississippi State instead of LSU. Charles always had to be a little bit different, you know." Then he frowned. "Hell, I'm using the past tense. Charles *has* to be a little bit different."

Nanette nodded, and gently placed her palm against Charles's. "Yeah, he's different, but in an incredibly good way. And we won't use past tense on anything. Charles *is* coming back. He has to."

16

SATURDAY SEEMED TO COME around quickly, with Nanette's week passing in a blur due to her visits to CCU, her teaching job, and the family's preparations for the plantation tours. After Chantelle's interview ran in the *Times-Picayune,* the smaller papers outside of Jefferson Parish also picked up the story, and Nanette had high hopes of proving to the historical society that their plantation was worthy of being saved.

She'd spent her entire Friday lunch hour on the phone with the National Register pleading her case and emphasizing the importance of a quick review of their addendum. Unfortunately, they'd said they were "extremely backed up with nomination packages," and would "process the addendum as soon as possible," with no indication of when that would be. But even so, Nanette still had high hopes that the National Register would deem the place worthy of historical-landmark status once they reviewed the packet. And she owed all of her newfound optimism to Charles.

She couldn't wait to tell him, as soon as she could. But even though he had improved some, as of that morning he still hadn't regained consciousness. Nanette, Johnny and the remainder of Charles's family had spent each day taking their respective turns passing through the CCU doors to see him during visiting hours. Maria, naturally, was also there at every opportunity. But Nanette didn't blame her for wanting him back; what woman wouldn't? However, she did blame Maria for trapping him with a lie and for keeping them apart way back when, essentially costing them years that they could have spent together.

Even so, she didn't confront Charles's ex-wife, but simply endured her visits to the hospital. Maria had no idea that Nanette knew what had really happened back then, and it wasn't Nan's place to tell her that she did. She suspected that only Charles himself would be able to dissuade his ex from her repeated claim that they'd been "so in love" and that they'd "somehow let that love slip away." Maria proclaimed to anyone who'd listen that she planned to rebuild their relationship as soon as he got better.

This morning, probably because it was Saturday and a nonworkday for most folks, there were plenty of Charles's extended family there, and Maria made sure each and every one of them heard her story. She played the pitiful wish-I-could-have-him-back ex-wife well. Nanette almost felt sorry for her. Almost. But mostly, she felt an extra surge of compassion for Charles, having to deal with Maria when he woke. It wouldn't be fun to see Barbie cry. Again. She'd cried a lot this week, particularly when she'd noticed anyone looking.

But Charles's ex wasn't what concerned Nanette. Charles was. Gage said that the only clear sign that Charles was truly recovering would be when he regained consciousness. So far that hadn't happened, and she couldn't get an exact answer out of her cousin regarding how long it should or shouldn't take. In other words, she didn't know if the fact that he'd now been in the CCU for eleven days was a bad thing. All Gage would say was that Charles's condition had steadily improved, even if only slightly.

Nanette knew his improvement was due to his absence from her bedroom and was sincerely grateful that he'd heeded her advice and stayed away to heal, even if she yearned for him so much every night that her body ached with desire. She smiled softly, looking forward to the day when they could act on that desire again.

She felt certain he'd recover, but the waiting wasn't easy. She wasn't exactly known for her patience. Thankfully, the open house today filled her hours between CCU visits with a steady stream of guests paying to walk through the Vicknair plantation in the hopes of viewing evidence of ghosts. Although no envelopes appeared on the tea service, the tourists still seemed impressed with the framed letters from John-Paul and Clara. And then, right before the last tour ended, Ryan's two ghosts came to continue their work on the attic. The folks touring the house at the time didn't seem overly convinced by the mere sounds of hammers or the creak of the ceiling as the ghosts moved around above them. So Ryan and Tristan opened the attic for viewing and took those who wanted a "real interaction with ghosts" up to see the hammers hovering in midair then batting at nails.

Nanette heard a few individuals comment that the floating hammers, nails and wood could have been done with invisible wires, but the majority of them seemed convinced.

The members of the historical society happened to arrive at the plantation house during that last tour, and even witnessed Ryan's ghosts in action. Nanette watched them eagerly, waiting to hear them say that they would back the plantation's right to stay standing, due to its connection to the spirit world and its ability to produce income based on that connection.

They didn't. Instead, one of the members, Paul Remondet, claimed that he wasn't certain that the place, haunted or not, would generate much public interest once the novelty wore off. "You've been in every paper this week," he said. "How many people do you think will show when this place is no different than any other plantation claiming to be haunted?"

Nanette was speechless, but Tristan wasn't. Evidently, he had gone to school with the guy and he held nothing back when he gave Remondet a piece of his mind. Unfortunately, that only seemed to make Remondet even more resolute.

"I'm afraid the place didn't make the cut, Tristan," he said firmly.

Nanette knew by merely looking at the intensity of Tristan's eyes and the hard set of his jaw that he wasn't done with Remondet yet. And she could almost sense the exact moment when he deemed him worthy of a good punch. Evidently, the oldest member of the society, Eddie Solomon, also saw Tristan's temper flaring, because he stepped between the two men and intervened.

"You know, Paul, I'm thinking that we should give the Vicknairs a little more time before we make the decision definite. They did send that addendum to the National Register this week, and I believe we should at least give them time to hear back from them and see if the house made landmark status." He looked at Nanette. "When did you mail the packet, Ms. Vicknair. Monday, wasn't it? That's when the copy was delivered to us at the society."

Nanette nodded. It was Monday, though with everything that had happened this week, Monday seemed a lifetime ago. "And I called the National Register yesterday. They're extremely backed up with nominations now, but promised that they'd review it as soon as possible."

"See the Register folks haven't even had it a week yet," Eddie said. "I say let's give them another week to respond. Will that work for you, Paul?"

"I don't think anything is going to change in that time, but sure, we can wait another week."

The Vicknairs stood on the front porch and silently watched the historical society members leave. Nanette didn't know what to say. She was shocked that some of their visitors had doubted the existence of ghosts even when they saw them firsthand, and now, although they'd put their secret out for the world to know, the society was still reluctant to fund the restoration.

"What got into you?" Chantelle broke the uncomfortable silence with the pointed question to Tristan. "I've never seen you so worked up."

"You should've seen him in high school," Dax said, and Tristan elbowed him.

"Maybe it's the fact that between work and the plantation, I haven't slept in two days, but he was being such a prick that I just wanted to hit him, and put me out of my misery." Tristan had come straight to the plantation after working all night at the firehouse and hadn't shown any sign of exhaustion…until now.

"Anyway," Tristan said, eyeing a laughing Dax as he

spoke, "I'm going to blame my lack of sleep for my lapse into caveman mentality. Paul isn't a bad guy, usually, but I didn't like what he was saying."

"Obviously," Monique said, smiling at her cousin.

"Well," Chantelle started, stepping toward her husband, "if you're blaming your lack of sleep for that, then I'll blame PMS for the fact that I rather liked it."

Everyone except Nanette laughed. She was too busy gathering her things and preparing to go back to the hospital.

"What do you think our chances are of hearing from the National Register by Monday?" Celeste asked.

"No idea," Dax said. "All we can do now is hope that they come through in time."

"Can you all finish cleaning up?" Nanette asked. Typically, she'd be in the middle of this conversation speculating on what would happen to their beloved home come Monday. But she had other things, more important things, on her mind right now. "I want to get to the hospital early."

"We can clean up," Jenee said, and the rest of the family echoed her statement.

"Thanks," Nanette called, already heading for her car.

Two weeks ago, she'd have spent the hour drive to the hospital reflecting about the open house, about the historical society, her family and whether or not they were about to lose their home. That'd been the primary thing on her mind since Katrina had hit—to save the home she loved. But she didn't think about that at all. She drove the entire way mentally repeating the same question that'd been on her mind for the past four days—would this be the day he woke up?

Entering the CCU waiting area, she found even more of Charles's family waiting to see him than there had been this morning. Johnny Roussel sat with his wife and kids, and he smiled at Nanette when she neared the waiting area. "Your cousin has good news."

Nan's heart sputtered in her chest, and she prayed it was the news she wanted. Then Johnny indicated the hallway, where Gage stood talking to Charles's parents. They lived in Lafayette, but even though they were well along in years, they'd driven over each day in the hopes of seeing their son.

"What kind of good news?" Nanette asked, her hopes building.

"Nanette." Gage apparently had seen her arrive and had come to tell her the "news" personally.

"Tell me he's awake, Gage."

"He is," Gage said, smiling, but quickly lifted his palm to halt her questions before she had a chance to begin. "However, I need to tell you the same thing I've told the family. I don't want to dampen your spirits, but you need to know that even though he's awake, he'll need to remain in CCU for us to keep an eye on him for a while. Also, he isn't talking quite yet. His throat is still raw from the ventilator, plus he's been on some strong meds and it will take time before they wear off enough for him to speak. So, while he'll be aware, he won't be communicating."

"But he's awake," she said, her emotions soaring. Charles was back, on this side. And soon, he'd be exactly where she wanted him to be, with her. "That's what matters."

"Exactly," he said, "but there's one more thing that I've asked everyone to consider, particularly since we have such a large crowd wanting to see him this morning. It's extremely important for Charles to stay calm now, so I'm asking all of those visiting him to limit their conversations, since it's naturally frustrating to have someone asking you questions when you're unable to answer. Also, keep whatever conversations you have with him to things that are positive." Gage spoke so everyone around them could hear, and Nanette knew this conversation was primarily for their benefit, so they could see she was receiving the same instructions that he'd given to them. Her cousin knew that she'd never say anything that wasn't positive to Charles. In fact, she couldn't wait to tell him that she positively loved him.

She smiled. "So can we see him now?"

"His parents have asked to go back first, then Johnny's family," Gage explained. "We're still limited to the two visitor rule for the CCU."

Nanette scanned the bounty of family members that filled the room to capacity. It wasn't only immediate family, but all of Charles's aunts, uncles, cousins, the whole shebang. If they all got to go back, then she might not be able to see him at all. Apparently, her consternation came through on her face, because Johnny cleared his throat and told Gage, "After my family, Nanette can go back. Then the rest of the Roussels."

"Thank you, Johnny." Ever since their conversation on Tuesday, when she told him that she'd actually seen Charles's spirit, Nanette had spoken with Johnny several times about her feelings for Charles. He was extremely supportive of the two of them, saying that Charles deserved to finally have the woman he'd always wanted. Nanette felt the same, but right now, she simply wanted to see him, to gaze into those smoky eyes and know that the two of them wouldn't waste any more time.

Nanette patiently waited while Charles's parents, and then Johnny's family, visited him. Then, when her turn came, Maria stood and started toward the CCU doors.

"Nanette is going back now, Maria," Johnny said, halting her progress.

"He can see two people at a time," Maria snapped, but Johnny again intervened. As she passed by, Nanette listened to him explain to Maria that she could go back next.

Everything in the CCU looked the same as it had all week, beeps filling the air, nurses working diligently, patients hidden behind curtain walls. But nothing about this morning was the same as any of the previous days. Behind the curtain enclosing room three, Charles was awake. Nanette fought the urge to run to that room, burst inside and kiss him, but she controlled that impulse, determined to do what Gage had said and remain calm, for Charles.

Pushing the curtain aside, she entered his room and saw those beautiful eyes, no longer the charcoal color they'd been when he'd come to her as a spirit, but the unique silvery gray she remembered. Those eyes followed her as she entered then sat on the stool beside the bed.

Charles's mouth quirked slightly.

"You made it back." Nanette smiled.

His brows dipped down in a frown.

"Sorry," she whispered. "It's just that, well, I'm very glad you're here. With me. On this side."

The frown intensified, with the corners of his mouth also turning down. He looked much better in appearance, his skin the familiar tan tone that she was accustomed to and the bruising on his face practically gone. The bandage that'd been covering the slash had been removed, and a thin line creased that side of his face, with only a few tiny pieces of medical tape placed along its length. Compared to before, he looked a hundred times better. Except for that frown.

"Charles?" she whispered, not wanting to upset him, but wanting to know what was bothering him now. "I wish I knew what was wrong."

He grimaced and coughed, the sound odd and gurgling.

"It's okay," she said. "Don't try to speak. Gage said it's too soon." She'd upset him, and she didn't even know what she'd done. "I'm going out, so some others can come back. You have a lot of family here to see you." She silently hoped Johnny had modified the visiting order, because she had a feeling seeing Maria right now might not be the best thing for him, if her own visit had somehow upset him.

She stood to leave then heard that wet gurgling sound again from the bed and turned.

"Sor-ry," he said, wincing through the word.

"Oh, Charles, you have nothing to be sorry about."

Another frown claimed his face, and he coughed again. "House," he whispered. "For your—house. The letter."

Nanette stood still. He was talking about the letter she'd received before his accident, before he went in the hospital, and before they'd been together, which meant...

He didn't remember anything that'd happened between them this week, didn't remember the two of them.

She swallowed thickly, prepared to tell him that they were saving the house, thanks to what he'd told them to do. But how could she tell him, if he didn't remember? Gage had said he didn't need to be upset. Learning that his spirit had visited Nanette, helped her family take the proper steps to save their home, and had repeatedly made love to her while his body was in the hospital, would probably upset him.

"Charles?" Maria's songlike voice echoed through the room as she pulled back the curtain, shot a look of loathing at Nanette and then plopped down on the stool Nanette had just vacated. "Oh, it's so good to see you awake, honey," she gushed, while Charles's gaze moved between the two women.

Obviously Johnny hadn't realized how surprising it'd be for his brother to find both Nanette and Maria here at the same time. Then again, Johnny had probably thought, like Nanette had, that Charles would remember his time in the middle with Nan, and therefore remember telling her about Maria and the past. But Charles didn't remember, and there was so much distress on his face now that it hurt Nanette to look at him.

"Ma-ria," he said, but he wasn't looking at his ex-wife; he was looking, apologetically, at Nanette.

"You're talking!" Maria gushed. "Oh, wow, he started talking," she told Nanette, "for me!"

Nanette wanted to hurl. And then pick up Barbie and toss her out of the room on her dainty little behind. But she wouldn't. Charles needed those around him to remain calm, and plus, Nan wouldn't know how to explain to him why she disliked Maria so much.

Meanwhile, he stared at Nanette as though trying to mentally tell her that his relationship with Maria was over. Nanette mouthed, "It's okay," but only received another look of confusion that pierced her heart. Finally she turned and left the room, believing he'd be less stressed with Maria alone than if she stayed and he had to try and figure out exactly what the two women knew about each other.

Gage stood near one of the other CCU rooms, and

Nanette walked toward him to tell him about Charles speaking, but Maria stuck her head out of the curtain and yelled, "He's speaking, Doctor. He spoke, for me!" Then she darted back into Charles's room. Gage closed the chart he was looking at and met Nanette.

"Charles spoke?" he asked.

"Yes. It looks as though it hurts him to do it, but he said a few words."

"Great. I'll go check on him now." He took a step toward Charles's room, but Nanette grabbed his arm and stopped his departure.

"Gage, he doesn't remember."

"Doesn't remember what? The accident? Because sometimes that happens, a person with head trauma will block out the moments right before the injury. That's not all that uncommon, and it could very well come back to him, eventually."

"No," she choked out. "I don't know whether he remembers the accident or not, but he doesn't remember me."

"He doesn't remember you at all?" Gage asked, a physician's concern clearly displayed in his tone.

She shook her head. "No, he remembers me. But he doesn't remember when he was with me in the middle. Everything we shared, everything we talked about. He doesn't remember." She peered toward his room and saw Maria exiting, a broad smile on her face. She moved through the CCU doors, and Nanette heard her yelling to the rest of Charles's family that he'd spoken, because of her.

"Nanette," Gage said softly. "Even if he can't remember what happened in the middle, the two of you can still start over again, now that you know how he really feels."

She nodded, her throat scratchy with emotion. "I know we can, but—" She recalled every moment he'd been with her, the way they'd opened up to each other, confessed their true feelings, from twelve years ago…and now. And the way they'd made love. "We shared something special."

Gage put an arm around her, nodded toward the next two Roussel family members who were making their way toward Charles's room, then asked, "Did you touch him?"

Nanette blinked. "Touch him?"

"When you were in his room just now. Did you touch him? Remember, that's what triggered Celeste's memory of when she was in the middle with Dax, his touch. Maybe in order for Charles to remember, you need to touch."

"I'd forgotten," she admitted. "I need to go back in, one more time before the visiting hour ends."

Gage looked at his watch, frowning. "The hour is nearly over, and there are still several more people trying to see him before it's done. And I can't let you in there after it ends."

"Just long enough to see if I can bring those memories back, Gage. I can't go through the night not knowing."

"Tell you what, after the couple that's in with him now leave, I'll let you go in—"

"Thank you," she interrupted.

"—but only for a few seconds, until the next two visitors come in. He's got a lot of people out there who've been concerned about him, too, and they want to see him, as well."

"I understand."

Nanette and Gage walked toward Charles's room, and a man and woman, probably an aunt and uncle, exited.

"Okay. Just until the next pair gets here," Gage said, holding the curtain open so Nanette could go in.

Charles looked much more tired now, as though the brief interactions with his family were exhausting him, but his eyes still zeroed in on Nanette when she entered, and he whispered, "Still mad?"

She smiled, moving toward the bed. "No." Then she placed her hand on his and waited, hoping, praying.

The curtain behind her opened and she knew that two more of his family members had entered, but she wouldn't turn from him now. She wanted to see the exact moment that he remembered that she loved him.

"You were, very mad," he said. "On—the phone."

Her eyes filled with tears she couldn't control. "I'm sorry I was so angry then, and I'm sorry about your accident, Charles," she said, starting over with the very words she'd said over a week ago, when she'd first found him in her bedroom. The past week was gone, lost and not retrievable with her touch. He didn't remember any of it, but Nanette would never forget.

Then the male part of the couple standing behind Nanette cleared his throat. "Hello, Charles. It's your cousin, John," he said, peeking around Nan to get closer to the bed. "And Odelle is here, too," he said, indicating the woman beside him.

"Hi, Charles," she said tenderly. "We're so glad you're doing better."

Charles managed to give them a hint of a smile, but then he looked back to Nanette. "We—need to talk."

She nodded and hated that she couldn't control her trembling chin. "Okay." Then, because she had no idea whether he now blamed her for the accident, she repeated, "I am sorry, Charles." She was sorry for the accident, but more than that, she was sorry for what she'd lost.

She left his room and the hospital, and went home, where she tried to remember the positive part of the day, that Charles was back on this side and could speak. And tried to control her sadness at the negative part, that the man she loved could no longer remember the most precious days of her life.

17

"WHAT DAY IS IT?" Charles asked the nurse. He'd regained his voice completely during the night, and he'd been trying to get someone—anyone—to talk to him ever since. He hadn't seen this nurse before, and he hoped she'd be more willing to answer his questions than the others had been.

"It's Sunday," she said softly, writing something on a chart as she checked the machines by the bed.

Good. This one talked. He'd been awake most of the night, and he was tired of just laying there watching the other nurses come and go without telling him anything. The night nurse had simply told him not to worry about anything and to rest. Rest? He'd been asleep for God knows how long and the thought of closing his eyes again wasn't even in the picture. What he wanted was out of here.

What he wanted…was Nanette.

He remembered seeing her last night, her face trembling and on the verge of tears as she told him she was sorry. Sorry. As though that accident was her fault. Sure, he'd been on the phone with her at the time of the wreck, but he'd swerved to keep from hitting that dog. That's what had caused the wreck, not Nanette and her hotter-than-hell temper.

He smiled. He'd never known another woman with the spunk to chew him out like that, and he liked it. Unfortunately, thinking of other women brought up thoughts of Maria, which reminded him of seeing her for the first time in years last night, in his room, with Nanette.

"Hell." What had Nanette heard about Charles's ex? He could only imagine what Maria told her, but he prayed that someone had told her the truth. Then again, he'd made his family swear to never talk about that time again, which made it even more surprising that they'd allowed Maria to come back and see him in CCU. He'd definitely have a word with Johnny about that lapse in better judgment.

"Something hurt?" the nurse asked.

Charles shook his head, knowing she misinterpreted his expletive. "No, nothing's hurt. Matter of fact, I feel fine. Ready to head home." He had several things to do, and he couldn't do them from this hospital bed. He needed to tell the historical society that they had to save the Vicknair plantation, if they hadn't already realized that on their own. And he needed to explain to Nanette that he'd never meant to have her home destroyed. For once, he was going to tell her the truth about the past.

Nearly losing his life made him realize that he'd been an idiot to play around with his feelings for her all this time. Next time he saw her, he wasn't going to give her a chance to argue. He was going to kiss her the way he had a couple of weeks ago, when they'd argued outside of her plantation house and he'd ended up grinding against her on his car. He grinned at the memory. And next time, he wasn't going to stop with a kiss. She'd wanted him. He'd felt it. And he'd make sure to give her everything she wanted... and then some.

"Let me guess. You're thinking about the blonde that's

been camped out in the waiting room all night," the nurse said, taking in Charles's face as he thought of Nanette.

The blonde. "No, I can promise you I definitely wasn't thinking about the blonde." He was thinking about the black-haired beauty who lived next door to his brother. But now he knew that Maria was in the waiting area. "Damn, she's staying here?"

"She's been here for days."

Which meant she'd talked to Nanette for days. He really needed to get out and rectify whatever mess Maria had caused this time. "Am I getting out of here soon?"

"You'll stay in CCU for another twelve hours, since the doctors like to watch you for at least a day after you've been unconscious for so long. And they may actually keep you in here longer, since it was nearly two weeks."

"Two? *Two* weeks?"

"Yes, two weeks tomorrow, in fact."

"You said it was Sunday."

"It is."

"But I didn't understand. I thought you meant last Sunday. If tomorrow makes two weeks, that means that this is the end of the month, and that tomorrow is the first."

"For someone who recently regained consciousness, you're on top of your game," she said with a smile.

The historical society had already met, twice, and had probably already assigned the demolition crews to the houses that were on the lower half of their list. And unless some miracle had happened, Nanette's house was in that number.

He saw her again, mouthing she was sorry. What did she have to be sorry for? He was the one that should be sorry.

He'd probably cost her family their beloved home, just because he'd been enjoying fighting with her about it.

"There was another woman here last night. She has black hair, and her name is Nanette."

"Nanette Vicknair," the nurse said. "I saw her here. She's Doctor Vicknair's cousin. I noticed she'd been here for all of your visits. Are you friends?"

Charles ignored the last part of her questions. They were more than friends, but it'd been a long time since she'd seen him as anything but an enemy. He'd remedy that soon. "Is Nanette out there now? Is she in the waiting area?"

She shook her head. "She wasn't the last time I checked, but the visiting time doesn't begin for another two hours. The blonde slept in the waiting room last night."

Charles wasn't surprised. Maria was the type who camped out for days at the ticket office when she wanted front row seats to a rock concert; in her whacked-out mind, she was probably camping out here to get dibs on the first visit. He really didn't want to have to deal with her again, but he also didn't want her filling Nanette's head with lies, something Maria was especially good at. "The woman in the waiting room. Is there any way I could see her before the visiting hour begins?"

The nurse frowned. "You know, that's why we call it the visiting hour, because *that's* when you can have visitors," she said, but her tone wasn't mean; it was sarcastic. She was having a bit of fun at his expense, and Charles didn't mind; it was nice to see that some of the nurses were human. Hell, most of her patients were probably unable to speak at all. Might as well let her have her fun with him.

"You know, you're in the wrong profession," he said. "You should do stand-up."

"I'll keep that in mind."

"So, can I see her before the visiting hour begins?"

"Highly unlikely. You'd need doctor approval, and there would have to be a really good reason to allow the public back here when it isn't visiting hours. It's for our patients' protection, you know, that we have limited access to the CCU."

"I'd like to speak to Dr. Vicknair," Charles said. Gage would understand what he wanted to do.

"Dr. Vicknair has the day off."

"Then I'd like to see whatever doctor doesn't have the day off," Charles said, imitating her sarcasm.

She grinned. "I really think you're fighting a lost cause here, since she can come back here in two hours, anyway."

"But I don't want her coming back here in two hours," Charles said. "I want her coming back here now, so I can get her to leave before the beginning of that visiting hour."

She looked shocked, and Charles said, "The blonde is my ex-wife. Now, can I please talk to the doctor?"

A nod of understanding passed between them, and then the nurse told him she'd be right back.

Charles waited, and in a few minutes a young doctor in green scrubs emerged from the other side of the curtain.

"I'm Dr. Simone. Hank Simone. Are you having problems?" the guy asked.

Charles smirked. "I'm in the Critical Care Unit, and I've lost nearly two weeks of my life. You tell me."

Dr. Simone looked to be in his late twenties, but when he smiled, a broad smile that seemed to extend fully into both cheeks, he could've been thirteen. "Okay, let me rephrase that," he said. "What problem are you having that I can help you with at the moment?"

"My ex-wife is out in the waiting area."

"And?"

"And I'd rather her not be."

"O-kay. Do you want me to ask her to leave?"

"No," Charles said. "No, I don't want to do that. She may not have been one of the brightest areas of my past, but I don't want to hurt her." If there was one word he could use to describe Maria, it was *fragile*. Charles didn't want to break her; he just wanted her to understand that there wasn't any way they were getting back together. And he needed to try to do that as nicely as possible, because he really wasn't in the mood for Maria's waterworks. No woman cried like Maria. She didn't merely cry; she dripped. Flowed. Poured.

"I see," the young doctor said. "You want to talk to her before everyone else arrives because you don't want to embarrass her?"

Charles nodded. That was pretty much it. And he didn't want her talking to Nanette any more than she'd already done.

"Okay, I'm not one to typically go about breaking the rules, but this seems to be an exception. I'll go get her, tell her to come back. But I'm limiting the visit to five minutes."

"Agreed."

Within minutes, Maria's tiny hand pushed the curtain aside and she entered, her pale blue eyes a little sleep-swollen, but otherwise, the picture of perfection.

"Charles," she whispered, stepping toward the bed and taking his hand in hers. She looked at him and her heart-shaped mouth instantly turned upside down and she shook her head. "Oh, honey, I'm so, so, sorry. Don't worry. I'll help you get through this. We'll do it together." She was talking very slow and very soft, as though afraid her words might hurt him.

"Maria, I'm fine."

Her eyes widened. "You're talking! I mean, you're really talking. Last night you said a few words, for me, but now, you—you sound normal again!"

"Thanks."

"No, that didn't come out right."

"It's okay, Maria. I get it," he said, remembering that she never was one for tact. "Listen, we need to talk. About us."

"I thought that you needed me now," she said hurriedly, and he knew she was trying to get the words out before he brought her back down to earth. "You do, you know. I could be a good wife to you now, Charles, and I could help you deal with all of this, like no one else can. Because I loved you, totally loved you, the way you were. And I still see you that way, no matter what."

"Maria," he tried again.

"I do. And I—well, I don't think other women would be able to do that. I've been in love with you ever since we were first together that spring so long ago. And I never wanted the marriage to end, you know that. I want us together, Charles. I want us to have everything we've always wanted."

"Maria, our marriage was based on a lie, and we never loved each other."

"I loved you, and that's the reason I did what I did," she said.

"Maria, we'd only been together twice when you said

you got pregnant. We hardly knew each other. How can you say…"

"I won't argue with you about it now," she said, and her sweet singsong voice had ventured over into accusatory territory, a tone he'd heard often throughout their short-lived marriage. If he so much as spoke to another female, she'd hit the roof. And she'd sounded…just like she sounded now.

"Maria, I appreciate you coming to see me. It does mean a lot to me. But the fact is, the two of us are not meant to have a future together."

"Because of Nanette, right?"

"I'm not going to talk to you about Nanette," he said. They'd done that plenty of times, too, during their marriage. Every time he'd taken too long to get home, she'd accused him of trying to squeeze in a drive to Louisiana to see Nan.

But now, he had a chance with Nanette, and he was going to take it, as soon as he got out of this damn hospital.

"Maria, like I said, I appreciate you coming, but I'm okay now."

"You think she'll even want you now?" Maria asked, and now he heard the tone that he'd heard toward the very end of their marriage, a sound he'd classify as pure venom.

"Maria, it's time for you to go."

"Fine, but I was willing to take you this way, because I can still look at you and see the way you looked before. I'm betting your pretty little Cajun won't be so forgiving. Then again, maybe she'll just make sure you always make love in the dark, so she doesn't have to look at your face." She turned, grabbed the curtain and slung it completely open, then stormed out of the CCU. Charles saw a bunch of nurses gathered around a desk nearby and attempting to act as though they hadn't heard their heated confrontation. He also saw the person he needed to talk to right now.

"Dr. Simone!" he yelled.

Hank Simone crossed the CCU, casually shut the curtain behind him and sat on the stool beside Charles's bed in what Charles assumed to be his bedside manner stance.

"I want to apologize for allowing her to come back. I know that you asked for her, but looking at the situation now, I realize that I shouldn't have agreed to it. I actually talked with her during the past week and didn't pick up on the fact that she's…"

"Three crawfish short of a pound," Charles said, and instantly recalled a time not too long ago when Nanette Vicknair had proclaimed the same thing about him.

Hank smiled, but it looked forced. Probably because he'd anticipated Charles's next question. Didn't matter. Charles was still going to ask it, and he wasn't going to be satisfied until he got a response.

"How bad is my face?"

Hank took a breath, then exhaled slowly. "All things considered, I'd say it's good."

"I've felt the bandages," Charles said, gingerly touching the tiny pieces of sticky fabric lining his left cheek and jaw. He hadn't really thought all that much about what they were covering. But Maria had. Apparently, even with the bandages in place, she could see what the end result was going to be. And it wasn't good.

"I want a mirror."

"Charles, your face is still healing. Right now, it looks much worse than it will after you've had time to heal."

"A mirror," Charles repeated. He'd never thought of himself as a vain person, but he couldn't deny that Maria's words had hit a nerve. There was a small part of him that was wondering how bad it was, and what Nanette would think of his new "look."

"Just a minute," the doctor said, leaving the room.

Charles waited, and instantly recalled the way Nanette had always looked at him, as though she thought he was the most gorgeous man alive. Even when she'd been spouting words of hate, Charles had seen the attraction. Her eyes always seemed to drink him in, the same way he was certain his eyes did her. He liked that fire between them. It was exciting, exhilarating, tempting.

What if she couldn't look at him that way again?

He instantly recalled last night, right before she'd left, when she'd told him she was sorry. He'd thought she was talking about the accident. Now, he wondered if she was apologizing for the results of that accident.

"Here you go. Like I said, you'll continue healing." Hank Simone reentered the curtained room.

Charles took the mirror, lifted it…and cringed.

His face had been sliced open, from just beneath his left eye all the way past his jaw. The bandages he'd felt were tiny white pieces of something that made the long stripe look akin to a single railroad track. He looked…broken.

And now, particularly after Maria's comments, he felt that way.

"I am sorry, Charles."

He wanted Nanette, but he didn't want her because of pity. Undoubtedly, she was trying to will herself into wanting him because she knew no one else would, and she felt like she was to blame for the accident that had left him looking this way.

"I do think you'll heal up quite nicely, once you've had more time," the doctor said, and Charles merely nodded.

"How long until the next visiting hour starts?" he asked.

"About an hour and a half," Hank said.

"But I don't have to see anyone if I choose not to, right?"

"Mr. Roussel—Charles—you've had plenty of visitors over the past few days, and all of them seemed very impressed with the way you are recovering."

"I didn't ask what they seemed impressed with," Charles said, curtly. "Let them know that I'm not seeing visitors. Not now, and not ever. And as soon as I can get out of here, I want to go home. Better still, see if you can get that approved for quicker rather than later."

Hank opened his mouth as if he was certain there was some procedure to fix this but he couldn't recall what it was, then simply nodded. "I'll do my best, Mr. Roussel."

"No visitors."

"I understand."

Charles waited for him to disappear behind the curtain, then he took another look in the mirror.

"I was willing to take you this way, because I can still look at you and see the way you looked before. I'm betting your pretty little Cajun won't be so forgiving. Then again, maybe she'll just make sure you always make love in the dark, so she doesn't have to look at your face."

He opened his fingers and let the mirror fall to the floor.

18

CHARLES HELD UP THE YELLOW flier and read it again. "I still don't understand what made the Vicknairs tell the world that they talk to ghosts," he said, as Johnny drove him home from the hospital. He was truly enjoying the freedom of being out of those medicinal-smelling walls. He'd been there for fifteen days, and it wouldn't bother Charles if he never went back. Way too many bad memories in that short span, even if he'd only been awake for the last three of those fifteen days.

"Well, *I* still don't believe you refused to let Nan see you at the hospital. You can't avoid her forever, Charles."

"Sure I can. I don't want, or need, her pity." Charles was certain Nanette had only visited because she felt like his injury was her fault, and although he did want her, he didn't want her that way.

"It isn't pity, and your face has started healing already. Like that doctor said this morning, it's unreal the difference from one day to the next. Hell, you might end up without even a scar if it keeps improving so much."

"I heard what he said, but even if it is healing, that's not the point."

"Then what is?"

"Nanette didn't come to see me because she wanted to. She did it because she felt obligated to. That's not good enough."

"And I'm telling you that you've pegged it wrong. She was there because she wants you."

"How would you know?" Charles asked, then before Johnny could answer—and because he was tired of talking about Nanette Vicknair—he reverted to the previous subject. "So, tell me the truth. Do you believe it?"

"Believe what?"

"That they're mediums for ghosts."

Johnny's mouth quirked slightly, and then he said, "I completely believe it."

"Well, that'll give them major points with the National Register, or it should. I called and talked to Paul this morning, but he said the historical society hasn't heard one way or the other whether they hit landmark status." Charles frowned. "Paul and Eddie gave them until this Saturday to learn something, but I'm hoping to convince them to give them longer. I wish Paul would actually listen to me, instead of just telling me to 'Feel better.' I never meant for their home to go down."

"I know," Johnny said, then apparently caught what Charles didn't say. "Wait a minute. When are you planning to try to convince them?" He glanced at his brother in the passenger seat. "Charles, you are *not* planning to go to that historical society meeting tonight, are you?"

"It is Tuesday, and I always go to that meeting on Tuesday nights. This one isn't any different."

"Hell, yeah, it is. You just got out of a two-week stay in the hospital, and I personally heard Gage tell you that the only reason he was letting you go is because you promised to take it easy at home—and not drive for another week."

"I lied."

"Well, I didn't. When I told him I'd make sure you adhered to those guidelines, I meant it. I'm dropping you off, and I'm taking your car keys."

"Last time I checked, I'm the older brother, and I distinctly remember that I'm the usual horse's behind of this duo. You can stop trying to be something you're not."

Johnny laughed. "You're staying home tonight."

"We'll see," Charles mumbled. He might not be willing to be around Nanette at the moment, but he was more than willing to help save her house. Then, after his face healed completely—and he agreed with Johnny that it was looking as though it would—he'd try to win her love again. Then he'd know it was because of him, and not because she felt like she'd ruined his face.

"Yeah," Johnny answered quietly. "We will see."

Charles started to ask him what he meant by that, but they'd arrived at his home, and he was too thrilled about being back to argue anymore. "Finally."

"I know you'll miss the bland hospital food and all, but we took the liberty of stocking your fridge with plenty of gumbo, jambalaya, étouffée and such."

"I've died and gone to heaven," Charles said, grinning.

"Truthfully, I just wanted to make sure you were stocked with groceries, because I knew you'd use that as an excuse to take off driving before you're supposed to."

"You're all heart, little brother."

"I try."

Charles climbed out, and Johnny grabbed the small duffel bag containing his things from the hospital, not a whole lot, since the majority of the time he hadn't been wearing anything but a hospital gown. He walked with

Charles to the front door, put the bag on a chair nearby and turned to go.

"What, you're not going to confiscate all my sets of car keys?" Charles asked, only half joking.

"Why bother. If you give me two sets, that just means you've got three. Give me three, that means there're four. There's no reason to pretend you're going to cooperate, but I have it under good authority that you won't be leaving your house tonight."

"What, did you drain the gas from my car?"

"No." Johnny smiled, then closed the door behind him on his way out, leaving Charles to wonder just what he'd cooked up to trap him in his own home.

He took a deep breath, turned…and saw exactly why Johnny believed he wouldn't be leaving. "Nanette."

She wore a black dress, the type that some women would classify as "simple" but on Nanette, it was anything but. The fabric molded against her breasts so that they were perfectly outlined, with just the right amount of cleavage on display, then it showcased her slim waist, curvy hips and killer legs. After his long stint in the hospital—or maybe just because of his long stint without Nanette—Charles was instantly hard.

Her eyes moved downward, and he knew she noticed. Like he could hide it.

"Nanette, what are you doing here?"

"I asked Johnny to let me welcome you home," she said, moving one hand to her shoulder, and gently pushing that side of the dress down. "And I asked the powers that be what I could do to help you remember." She shrugged, and the action caused the other side of the dress to fall to the opposite elbow, so that the entire top portion rested midway down her torso, and a sheer—very sheer—black nightie underneath was now on display.

Amazingly, Charles grew harder. *Mon Dieu,* no one affected him like Nanette. Even so, her words didn't make sense, and he really wanted to understand what was happening here. "The powers that be?"

"On the other side. I'm a medium, you know. So I wrote them a note and left it on the tea service—that's how we communicate. They wrote back, and said I needed to do something to spark your memory," she said, shifting her hips to let the dress fall completely to the floor. Then she stepped out of it, and he was treated to an erotic vision of Nanette Vicknair, wearing nothing but that sexy black nightie and stilettos. He couldn't have produced a better image if he tried.

I'm a medium, you know.

Her words finally got to his brain, quite a feat, since his brain was rather muddled at the moment. "I didn't know you were a medium until Johnny showed me the flier on the way over."

She paused, one side of that full mouth easing down—for just a second, but he noticed—then she said, "Charles, you already knew. And I'm going to help you remember exactly when you found out. In fact, I'm going to help you remember everything, and then, I want…"

"You want what, Nanette?"

"I want you, forever."

He'd craved hearing her say those words for longer than he remembered, but they had no meaning now, not until she was no longer blaming herself for his scar. Sending her away seemed absolutely impossible, especially in his current aroused state, but no matter how much he wanted Nanette, he didn't want her pity.

He wanted her love.

"Nanette, you need to go," he said, trying his best to keep his voice firm, commanding. "Now."

Her green eyes blinked in surprise. No doubt. What man in his right mind would send her away, looking like a centerfold and doing her best to seduce him? Then again, at the moment, Charles didn't exactly feel like he was in his right mind. In fact, this seemed like a dream. And he could almost recall a similar dream, with Nanette wearing this nightie at another place, another time.

He shook his head, trying to separate the two images, but they were so similar that it was difficult. "You need to go."

"You're starting to remember, aren't you?"

"Remember what, Nanette? The phone call before the wreck? Yeah, I remember, but the accident wasn't your fault. Surely by now you've heard what happened. A dog ran out in front of me, I swerved, and the next thing I knew, I was in the hospital. That was it. It wasn't anything that you could have—" His words stilled in his throat as she pushed one strap of the nightie down, and then the other, and unlike the dress, this piece of clothing didn't make any stops on its way to the floor.

"Nanette," he said, his voice as raspy as it had been when he'd first spoken at the hospital. "What are you trying to do to me? I—I don't want your pity, *chère*."

"This has nothing to do with pity, and everything to do with desire. And with how much I want you, and how much you want me. How much you've wanted me for the past twelve years."

He swallowed. He hadn't told her about the past twelve years, and even if Maria had, she damn sure wouldn't have told Nanette that he'd never gotten over her.

"I've wanted you for that entire time, too," she whispered, moving closer to him with every word.

Charles's penis pressed against his jeans, and he literally sensed what it would feel like to lose his clothes and sink himself deep, deep into her. He could almost feel it, the way her intimate walls would clench around him, and he swore he could hear the way she'd scream his name. He closed his eyes, and saw it happen. When had he had such a vivid dream?

"Kiss me, Charles."

"Nanette, I don't want you until you really want me. You're feeling guilty about this," he said, taking a finger to the thin line that creased his face. "But it will heal, and I don't want you, not that way. If we're together again—no, when we're together again, because it will happen—it'll be because you want to and not because of this."

"Kiss me, Charles," she repeated, pulling his shirt from his pants, then pushing it over his head and dropping it to the floor. She wrapped her arms around his neck, tunneled her fingers into his hair, then pushed her full breasts against his chest. "Kiss me, please."

"*Chère,* how am I supposed to say no to this?"

"You're not," she whispered, her warm breath feathering across his lips.

Charles was tired of fighting, and he was tired of always wanting…this. He edged his mouth to hers, traced her lips with his tongue, eased it inside and his mind immediately flooded with visions…

She was on her bed, her hands on black panties, then she pushed them to the floor. "Please, inside me, now!" she cried, and he nudged her legs apart with his thigh and plunged inside, deep, deep inside, while she yelled his name.

"Charles, I've missed you," she panted, and Charles blinked, then realized that he was now as naked as she, and that her hands were clawing his chest while she worked hot kisses down his abdomen.

"Can I taste you now?" she asked him in the dream.

Then the memory became reality as she closed her mouth over his penis, and Charles nearly lost it before they'd even really started.

"Nanette, we've—we've done this, haven't we?"

"Mmm-hmm," she answered, the mumbled acknowledgment vibrating against his length as she took him into her throat.

Charles was having a difficult time focusing on what was a dream—no, not a dream, a memory—and what was real. Images flooded his mind of the two of them sharing, laughing, loving and talking about…how he needed to get back to this side.

"I—don't get it," he said, his head foggy from trying to figure it out while her tongue was lapping at his balls.

"But you're remembering, aren't you?" she asked, then blew a stream of cool air along his length as she eased her way back up his body.

"Yeah, I'm remembering."

"Good," she said, then took his hand and led him through his house to his bedroom. She climbed on the bed and put her hands on the headboard, grabbing on to the wood. "Let me feel it again, Charles."

Again. They had done this before. He saw her, clasping her headboard because…she wasn't allowed to touch.

"Mediums aren't allowed to touch spirits," he said. "I was a ghost." It wasn't really a question.

"But we did make love, Charles. Because I wanted to, I wanted you. The same way I want you now. And it had nothing at all to do with any wreck, or any scar, or anything except how much I want you, how much I've always wanted you."

He moved behind her on the bed, slid his hands around to massage her breasts and knew that he *had* made love to her like this, just like this, and it hadn't been that long ago. No more than two weeks ago, for sure.

"How could I have forgotten?" he asked, losing himself in the exquisiteness of touching her, feeling her, loving her. He slid his palms down her abdomen to her thighs and eased them apart, then glided a hand to her center, his thumb massaging her clit while his fingers delved into her wet heat.

His penis pushed against her, and she shifted her hips to help guide where she wanted him to go.

"I want you to come first," he said, thrilled at the realization that Nanette did want him, that she'd always wanted him. He could hear her telling him that now, hear her saying that she'd never wanted anyone else. It had always been him. Always been Charles.

"I'll come with you inside," she begged. "Please, Charles, I can't wait anymore. I need you in me."

He withdrew his fingers and replaced them with his penis. She was hot and wet and ready, and she wasn't going to let him take this easy. She grasped the headboard and pushed against him, so that Charles had no choice but to give her everything. He pushed back, giving her everything she wanted, while her frantic gasp filled the room.

"Oh, *chère,* I didn't mean to hurt you," he said, attempting to hold himself still to keep from causing her any additional pain.

"It'll only hurt," she said, panting through the words, "if you stop!"

Fierce, possessive desire filled him with her command, and he gave her what she wanted, pushing deep within her while she met him thrust for thrust, the sounds of their passion filling the bedroom as each and every detail of his time in between confirmed the fact that what they were doing now had nothing to do with pity, nothing to do with guilt and everything to do with…love.

19

"THEREFORE, MY RECOMMENDATION is that the historical society allow the Vicknair plantation to remain as a symbol of Louisiana heritage, proof that the state embodies a spirit like none other, the spirit of the living and of the dead. And I'm proof that the place is what it claims, since I happened to visit this place when I was hovering between this side, and the next," Charles said to the historical society, as they gathered in Adeline Vicknair's sitting room.

The society had hung around the plantation throughout the day to view the Saturday tours and to conduct a thorough inspection. Charles had been a part of the group, but unfortunately, due to his "recent relationship with a member of the Vicknair family," as Paul Remondet had put it, the remainder of the committee felt that President Roussel shouldn't have the final say. Charles had understood that, sort of, but even so, his argument held merit. Though the Vicknairs hadn't received word from the National Register yet, the fact that they were a stopping point for ghosts on their way to the light deemed the house worthy to remain standing, in Charles's opinion.

However, standing next to Nanette and the remaining members of the Vicknair family, and listening to the rest of the society's discussions on the other side of the room, Charles was beginning to think he was fighting a losing battle.

"Surely they're not going to turn us down now," Monique Vicknair said, rubbing her swollen belly as she spoke. "Are they, Charles? I mean, they know now that you are proof that we help spirits stuck in the middle."

"You'd think there wouldn't be any need for discussion, huh, honey?" Nanette said, wrapping an arm around him.

Charles was having a hard time feeling bad about the situation, because he felt so damn good with her by his side. But he wanted her to have the house and he wanted the Vicknairs to keep helping spirits. What would've happened to him if Nanette hadn't sent him back to reunite with his body? He might've roamed the middle for years.

He smirked. Reunite with his body. Something mighty strange about even thinking that.

"Oh, my, look!" Wendy Millwood exclaimed, pointing to the silver tea service, where a small lavender piece of paper had just appeared.

"That's the way we get our assignments," Monique said, in a "See, we told you so" tone that was probably a little stronger due to her pregnancy hormones.

Nanette moved toward the tea service and picked up the paper. "But this isn't an assignment. It's a note." She turned it over, read it.

"What's it say?" Wendy asked, and everyone in the room became silent waiting for her answer.

"It's from Grandma Adeline. She says to check the mail."

"Come on," Charles said, grabbing Nanette's hand and leading her down the stairs and out to the mailbox. The rest of her family and the society members also came out of the house and stood at the front porch waiting to see what was important enough to warrant a note from Nanette's dead grandmother.

"What do you think?" Nanette asked, opening the box.

"I have an idea," he said, "but just look and see."

Sure enough, as she thumbed through the letters, one stood out from the rest, primarily because of the return address, from the National Register of Historic Places. "Oh, Charles, what do you think? Would they send a letter if they were turning us down?"

"Chère," he said softly.

"Yeah?"

"Open it and see."

She did, withdrew the single sheet inside and then collapsed against him, her tears falling steadily. *Mon Dieu,* he prayed they hadn't said no.

"Nanette?" he questioned.

"We did it, Charles," she whispered, then she looked up at him, her green eyes wet, but beaming with excitement. "We did it, because of you. You told me what to do, and then we all worked together to do it, and now…we're on the list!" She held up the paper.

"Well?" Gage yelled from the porch.

"Yeah, tell us something!" Tristan followed.

"Hey, I'm liable to go into labor before you let us know. Come on, Nan!" Monique bellowed.

"We did it!" Nanette screamed back, hugging Charles and then hurrying back toward the house with him at her side. "Listen. Listen to this," she said, barely able to speak she was so ecstatic. "I am pleased to inform you that the Vicknair plantation has been added to the

National Register of Historic Places with National
Landmark Status."

Charles looked up as she read to see Nanette's entire
family huddled together, crying, laughing, cheering.
They'd done it. They'd saved their home. Saved their
family. A family that, in his mind, was already his, too.

But he needed to make that official, as well. "Nanette,"
he said, wanting to add even more excitement to this
perfect day. "Marry me." He realized it wasn't really a
question, but she knew he wasn't the type to ask for what
he wanted. He was the type to demand it. And what he
wanted, more than anything he'd ever wanted in his life,
was Nanette. "Please, *chère*. Say yes."

"Yes!" she gushed. "Oh, yes, Charles!"

He picked her up and swung her around, ignoring
Gage's warning from the porch about overexertion. "I'll
exert if I want," Charles said. "I just asked your cousin to
marry me, and she said…yes!"

Epilogue

Four weeks later

"CAN YOU BELIEVE HOW QUICKLY they got everything done?" Nanette asked her husband, as they stood beneath the big oak in front of the plantation home, which was now totally restored and truly exceptional.

"Can't really be surprised at that," Charles said. "Lots of people make things happen quickly, when they finally get things right, Mrs. Roussel." The two of them sure had, having a small family wedding two weeks ago, because they simply didn't want to wait.

She kissed him in the same spot she always did, on what she called his "devil's dimple." Then she traced the tiny line, nearly invisible, but still there enough for her to see it, and to say it reminded her of how she'd finally gotten the man she loved. "So glad we finally got things right," she said, kissing her way down that line, then ending with his lips.

He smiled, hugging her. "Me, too."

She looked back at the plantation home. "It's so hard to believe. They fixed the columns, fixed the right side, fixed everything."

"Once the National Register deems a place worthy of

landmark status, they're going to do whatever it takes to make sure that landmark is preserved. And in your case, preserved for the masses to enjoy." He smiled as yet another bus parked on the large piece of land Johnny had designated as "haunted plantation tour parking."

Charles's brother had offered a portion of his land to the new venture, and his daughter Cindy had been thrilled. Now she worked every Saturday taking parking money, a much easier job, she said, than dealing with all of the crazy people that called Charles's office upset about one thing or another.

"Look at that line for her book," Nanette said, pointing to a table at one end of the porch where Chantelle was busily signing her newest release, the true account of the Vicknair family history.

"Do you think they're in line for the book, or for the ghost?" Charles asked, grinning. Ryan had had two ghosts show up today, but since all of the construction work had been completed by the restoration folks, they'd had to find other things to do. One of them had decided to hand Chantelle's autographed books to purchasers, and they squealed with delight when a book levitated in midair before being placed in their hands.

"It's probably a bit of both," Nanette said.

They greeted guests, answered questions and visited with the rest of the family throughout the day, while over two hundred people toured their home. Because it was "their" home now.

With all of the other cousins already having houses of their own, they'd all agreed that Nanette and Charles should take over full-time residency at the plantation.

Charles had been almost as thrilled as Nanette with their decision. They'd be in the house Nanette loved, and he'd also be close to his brother and his family. And they'd start a family of their own, soon.

"When do you want to tell them our news?" he asked, kissing her cheek as they watched the last of the tourists leave.

"I've been dying to tell them all day," Nanette said. "Let's not wait any longer."

Charles prepared to yell for the family to gather on the porch, but, as usual, his wife's impatience won the race.

"Hey, everyone, come here! We've got news!" she yelled.

He snuggled her close, then laughed against her hair. "Do you think maybe I can be the one to tell them if it's a boy or a girl, when we know, I mean?"

"Only if you beat me to it," she said, and he knew there wasn't a chance of that happening.

"Good thing I love you, *chère.*"

"Good thing I love you, too," she countered, while the porch filled with Vicknairs eager to hear their news.

"Okay, we're all here," Tristan said. "What's up?"

"You wanna tell them?" she asked him, and Charles grinned. There was no way he'd take her fun away now.

"You go ahead, *chère.*"

"What is it?" Jenee asked.

"Well, we figure since we've got this big ol' house to live in, we might as well get started filling it up," Nanette said. "We're having a baby!"

The cheers and yells from the porch were earsplitting, and Charles loved it, laughing with Nanette at their excitement.

"*Mon Dieu,* we're not wasting any time getting this next

generation of Vicknairs going, are we?" Gage asked, and he leaned down and kissed Kayla's belly, not quite as large as Monique's, but getting there.

"When are you due?"

"I'm due the second week of May. I'm in my seventh week!" Nanette said excitedly.

Again, more cheers, more squeals, and then…the realization that Charles and Nanette were both waiting for.

"Wait a minute," Gage said. "Wait one minute."

Nanette looked at Charles, smiled. "What is it?"

"Seven weeks? Seven weeks ago, Charles was in my care, at the hospital, and quite unconscious at the time."

"Right," Nanette said, grinning bigger now.

"No way!" Monique gasped.

"What?" Ryan asked, and Monique elbowed him.

"Don't you get it?" she asked. "She got pregnant when he was a spirit!"

"No, surely you couldn't get pregnant from being together in the middle," Chantelle said, but she was grinning. "Well, let me tell you, I certainly haven't portrayed *that* in my books."

Nanette laughed. "Obviously, we still have plenty to learn about what happens in the middle. But, hey, if we don't figure it all out, maybe the next generation will." She clasped her hand with Charles's, then placed it over her belly, over their child.

Monique shrieked, but it wasn't an excited shriek. It sounded like a shriek of…pain.

"Honey, what it is?" Ryan asked.

"It's that next generation, ready to get started," she

said, looking from Ryan to the rest of her family. "My water just broke!"

"Have mercy, let's go!" Ryan said. "Let's go, everyone!" He carefully maneuvered Monique toward her car while the rest of the family scattered across the yard to climb in their vehicles and head toward the hospital, a place that, several weeks ago, Charles had vowed never to enter again. But he now realized that hospitals weren't merely for those who were fighting death; they were also a place for giving life.

And death wasn't what it seemed, either. The incredibly warm light waiting to welcome those who were ready to pass through wasn't anything to fear, but something to look forward to. When it was his time.

But now wasn't his time, not yet. For now, he'd stay put, greeting the first Vicknair of the next generation of mediums, loving the woman he'd always wanted, raising the baby that they'd bring into the world soon.

For now, he'd go toward a different light…the light of life.

* * * * *

Turn the page for a sneak preview of
AFTERSHOCK, *a new anthology*
featuring New York Times *bestselling author*
Sharon Sala.

Available October 2008.

n●cturne ™

Dramatic and sensual tales of paranormal romance.

Chapter 1

October
New York City

Nicole Masters was sitting cross-legged on her sofa while a cold autumn rain peppered the windows of her fourth-floor apartment. She was poking at the ice cream in her bowl and trying not to be in a mood.

Six weeks ago, a simple trip to her neighborhood pharmacy had turned into a nightmare. She'd walked into the middle of a robbery. She never even saw the man who shot her in the head and left her for dead. She'd survived, but some of her senses had not. She was dealing with short-term memory loss and a tendency to stagger. Even though she'd been told the problems were most likely temporary, she waged a daily battle with depression.

Her parents had been killed in a car wreck when she was twenty-one. And except for a few friends—and most recently her boyfriend, Dominic Tucci, who lived in the apartment right above hers, she was alone. Her doctor kept reminding her that she should be grateful to be alive, and on one level she knew he was right. But he wasn't living in her shoes.

If she'd been anywhere else but at that pharmacy when the robbery happened, she wouldn't have died twice on the way to the hospital. Instead of being grateful that she'd survived, she couldn't stop thinking of what she'd lost.

But that wasn't the end of her troubles. On top of everything else, something strange was happening inside her head. She'd begun to hear odd things: sounds, not voices— at least, she didn't think it was voices. It was more like the distant noise of rapids—a rush of wind and water inside her head that, when it came, blocked out everything around her. It didn't happen often, but when it did, it was frightening, and it was driving her crazy.

The blank moments, which is what she called them, even had a rhythm. First there came that sound, then a cold sweat, then panic with no reason. Part of her feared it was the beginning of an emotional breakdown. And part of her feared it wasn't—that it was going to turn out to be a permanent souvenir of her resurrection.

Frustrated with herself and the situation as it stood, she upped the sound on the TV remote. But instead of *Wheel of Fortune,* an announcer broke in with a special bulletin.

"This just in. Police are on the scene of a kidnapping that occurred only hours ago at The Dakota. Molly

Dane, the six-year-old daughter of one of Holly-
wood's blockbuster stars, Lyla Dane, was taken by
force from the family apartment. At this time they
have yet to receive a ransom demand. The house-
keeper was seriously injured during the abduction,
and is, at the present time, in surgery. Police are
hoping to be able to talk to her once she regains consciousness. In the meantime, we are going now to a
press conference with Lyla Dane."

Horrified, Nicole stilled as the cameras went live to
where the actress was speaking before a bank of micro-
phones. The shock and terror in Lyla Dane's voice were
physically painful to watch. But even though Nicole kept
upping the volume, the sound continued to fade.

Just when she was beginning to think something was
wrong with her set, the broadcast suddenly switched from
the Dane press conference to what appeared to be footage
of the kidnapping, beginning with footage from inside the
apartment.

When the front door suddenly flew back against the
wall and four men rushed in, Nicole gasped. Horrified, she
quickly realized that this must have been caught on a
security camera inside the Dane apartment.

As Nicole continued to watch, a small Asian woman,
who she guessed was the maid, rushed forward in an effort
to keep them out. When one of the men hit her in the face
with his gun, Nicole moaned. The violence was too remi-
niscent of what she'd lived through. Sick to her stomach,
she fisted her hands against her belly, wishing it was over,
but unable to tear her gaze away.

When the maid dropped to the carpet, the same man followed with a vicious kick to the little woman's midsection that lifted her off the floor.

"Oh, my God," Nicole said. When blood began to pool beneath the maid's head, she started to cry.

As the tape played on, the four men split up in different directions. The camera caught one running down a long marble hallway, then disappearing into a room. Moments later he reappeared, carrying a little girl, who Nicole assumed was Molly Dane. The child was wearing a pair of red pants and a white turtleneck sweater, and her hair was partially blocking her abductor's face as he carried her down the hall. She was kicking and screaming in his arms, and when he slapped her, it elicited an agonized scream that brought the other three running. Nicole watched in horror as one of them ran up and put his hand over Molly's face. Seconds later, she went limp.

One moment they were in the foyer, then they were gone.

Nicole jumped to her feet, then staggered drunkenly. The bowl of ice cream she'd absentmindedly placed in her lap shattered at her feet, splattering glass and melting ice cream everywhere.

The picture on the screen abruptly switched from the kidnapping to what Nicole assumed was a rerun of Lyla Dane's plea for her daughter's safe return, but she was numb.

Before she could think what to do next, the doorbell rang. Startled by the unexpected sound, she shakily swiped at the tears and took a step forward. She didn't feel the glass shards piercing her feet until she took the second step. At that point, sharp pains shot through her foot. She gasped, then looked down in confusion. Her legs looked as if she'd been running through mud, and she was standing in broken glass and ice cream, while a thin ribbon of blood seeped out from beneath her toes.

"Oh, no," Nicole mumbled, then stifled a second moan of pain.

The doorbell rang again. She shivered, then clutched her head in confusion.

"Just a minute!" she yelled, then tried to sidestep the rest of the debris as she hobbled to the door.

When she looked through the peephole in the door, she didn't know whether to be relieved or regretful.

It was Dominic, and as usual, she was a mess.

Nicole smiled a little self-consciously as she opened the door to let him in. "I just don't know what's happening to me. I think I'm losing my mind."

"Hey, don't talk about my woman like that."

Nicole rode the surge of delight his words brought. "So I'm still your woman?"

Dominic lowered his head.

Their lips met.

The kiss proceeded.

Slowly.

Thoroughly.

* * * * *

Be sure to look for the
AFTERSHOCK *anthology next month,*
as well as other exciting paranormal stories
from Silhouette Nocturne.
Available in October wherever books are sold.

Silhouette®

SPECIAL EDITION™

FROM *NEW YORK TIMES* BESTSELLING AUTHOR

LINDA LAEL MILLER

A STONE CREEK CHRISTMAS

Veterinarian Olivia O'Ballivan finds the animals in Stone Creek playing Cupid between her and Tanner Quinn. Even Tanner's daughter, Sophie, is eager to play matchmaker. With everyone conspiring against them and the holiday season fast approaching, Tanner and Olivia may just get everything they want for Christmas after all!

Available December 2008
wherever books are sold.

Harlequin® Historical
Historical Romantic Adventure!

HALLOWE'EN HUSBANDS

With three fantastic stories by

Lisa Plumley
Denise Lynn
Christine Merrill

Don't miss these unforgettable stories about three women who experience the mysterious happenings of Allhallows Eve and come to discover that finding true love on this eerie day is not so scary after all.

Look for
HALLOWE'EN HUSBANDS

Available October
wherever books are sold.

Romantic
SUSPENSE

**Sparked by Danger,
Fueled by Passion.**

USA TODAY bestselling author

Merline Lovelace

Undercover Wife

Secret agent Mike Callahan, code name Hawkeye,
objects when he's paired with sophisticated
Gillian Ridgeway on a dangerous spy mission
to Hong Kong. Gillian has secretly been in love
with him for years, but Hawk is an overprotective
man with a wounded past that threatens to
resurface. Now the two must put their lives—
and hearts—at risk for each other.

Available October wherever books are sold.

REQUEST YOUR FREE BOOKS!

2 FREE NOVELS
PLUS 2
FREE GIFTS!

HARLEQUIN®

Blaze™

Red-hot reads!

HB08R

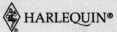

COMING NEXT MONTH

#423 LETHAL EXPOSURE Lori Wilde
Perfect Anatomy, Bk. 3
Wanting to expand her sexual IQ, Julie DeMarco selects Sebastian Black—hotshot PR exec—to participate in a no-strings fling. The playboy should be an easygoing love-'em-and-leave-'em type, but what if there's more to the man than just his good looks?

#424 MS. MATCH Jo Leigh
The Wrong Bed
Oops! It's the wrong sister! Paul Bennet agrees to take plain Jane Gwen Christopher on a charity date only to score points with her gorgeous sister. So what is he thinking when he wakes up beside Gwen the very next morning?

#425 AMOROUS LIAISONS Sarah Mayberry
Lust in Translation
Max Laurent thought he was over his attraction to Maddy Green. But when she shows up on the doorstep of his Paris flat, it turns out the lust never went away. He's determined to stay silent so as not to ruin their friendship—until the night she seduces him, that is.

#426 GOOD TO THE LAST BITE Crystal Green
Vampire Edward Marburn has only one goal left—to take vengeance on Gisele, the female vamp who'd stolen his humanity. Before long, Edward has Gisele right where he wants her. And he learns that the joys of sexual revenge can last an eternity....

#427 HER SECRET TREASURE Cindi Myers
Adam Carroway never thought he'd agree to work with Sandra Newman. Hit the sheets with her...absolutely. But work together? Still, his expedition needs the publicity her TV show will bring. Besides, what could be sexier than working out their differences in bed?

#428 WATCH AND LEARN Stephanie Bond
Sex for Beginners, Bk. 1
When recently divorced Gemma Jacobs receives a letter she'd written to herself ten years ago in college, she never guesses the contents will inspire her to take charge of her sexuality, to unleash her forbidden exhibitionist tendencies...and to seduce her totally hot, voyeuristic new neighbor....

HBCNM0908